What if something happened to his nephew?

The double door swung open at the end of the lobby and a flurry of both uniformed and plainclothes officers from the Missing Person's Unit rushed through.

But Justin only had eyes for one—Corporal Violet Jones. She wore a crisp black blazer, with her bright gold badge hanging on a lanyard. Her gait was steady. Then her remarkable indigo eyes met his through rectangular glasses and she faltered a step.

"Justin!" she called. "What are you doing here?"

Those were the first words he'd heard her say to him since the day he'd called off their engagement.

"Sadie just had a baby."

Sadness washed over her features and fear clutched his heart.

She nodded to the guard in front of him. "Let him through."

"Thank you," Justin called. But she'd already disappeared through another door. He bolted up the stairs to the maternity ward. But it was too late. Uniformed police officers gathered around the door to his sister's room. Her heartbreaking cries echoed down the hall.

His newborn baby nephew had been kidnapped.

Maggie K. Black is an award-winning journalist and romantic suspense author with an insatiable love of traveling the world. She has lived in the American South, Europe and the Middle East. She now makes her home in Canada with her history-teacher husband, their two beautiful girls and a small but mighty dog. Maggie enjoys connecting with her readers at maggiekblack.com.

Books by Maggie K. Black

Love Inspired Suspense

Undercover Protection
Surviving the Wilderness
Her Forgotten Life
Cold Case Chase
Undercover Baby Rescue

Pacific Northwest K-9 Unit

Undercover Operation

Rocky Mountain K-9 Unit

Explosive Revenge

Protected Identities

Christmas Witness Protection
Runaway Witness
Witness Protection Unraveled
Christmas Witness Conspiracy

Visit the Author Profile page at LoveInspired.com for more titles.

Undercover Baby Rescue

Maggie K. Black

LOVE INSPIRED SUSPENSE
INSPIRATIONAL ROMANCE

LOVE INSPIRED® SUSPENSE
INSPIRATIONAL ROMANCE

ISBN-13: 978-1-335-59782-3

Undercover Baby Rescue

Copyright © 2023 by Mags Storey

Recycling programs
for this product may
not exist in your area.

For questions and comments about the quality of this book, please contact us at CustomerService@Harlequin.com.

Love Inspired
22 Adelaide St. West, 41st Floor
Toronto, Ontario M5H 4E3, Canada
www.LoveInspired.com

Printed in U.S.A.

Fear thou not; for I am with thee: be not dismayed;
for I am thy God: I will strengthen thee;
yea, I will help thee; yea, I will uphold thee
with the right hand of my righteousness.
—*Isaiah* 41:10

To everyone at the gym who puts up with the fact
I talk to myself during workouts because my characters
won't be quiet long enough to let me finish my burpees.

You bring so much happiness and strength into my life
and I'm endlessly thankful for you.

ONE

Officer Justin Leacock of the RCMP's National Cyber-crime Unit was no stranger to the feeling that, with every move he made, he held the lives of innocent people in his hands. But as he stood in his half sister's hospital room in Vancouver, British Columbia, and cradled his new-born baby nephew in his arms, an urgent, deep and un-expected sense of responsibility ached within his chest.

Dear Lord, please help me be a good uncle. Help me protect him with my life.

Heavy January snow buffeted against the outside window. A lump formed in Justin's throat. His nephew was tiny and perfect. The child's eyes were scrunched closed in sleep. His little head nestled against Justin's shoulder, and his toes brushed against his forearm. The kid would never know just how many of Justin's answered prayers had led to this moment. The baby's mother, Sadie, was barely nineteen and struggled with addiction and homelessness. The baby's father was dead.

"But here you are," Justin whispered. "Healthy, safe and loved."

Gingerly he eased his phone from his pocket and silently snapped a selfie of them both. Justin glanced at the screen and grimaced. His dark blond hair was scruffy, and he was three days overdue for a shave. Well, he could always crop himself out.

"Justin?" Sadie's voice came from behind him. "Promise me you'll never tell anyone who his father was. Ever."

Justin turned back. His little sister was struggling to sit up against large white pillows that seemed to dwarf her skinny frame. Sadie was ten years younger than him, and he hadn't even known she existed until Sadie had approached him at his father's funeral two years ago and asked him for money.

"Hey, you, I didn't realize you were awake." He set the baby down in the bassinet beside Sadie's bed. "Do you want me to help you sit up?"

Sadie nodded, then she leaned against his left arm while he propped the pillows up behind her back with his right.

"The nurse told me I don't have to put the dad's name on the birth certificate if I don't know who he was," Sadie said. "Only I do know. But he's dead now. Lee died before I even knew I was pregnant."

Justin felt his jaw clench. Lee had been a drug dealer and killer who'd taken the lives of several people, including two incredibly brave local police officers, before an officer's bullet had ended his. Justin had failed to protect Sadie from getting involved with him. But he'd do everything in his power to protect her now.

"I think it's okay if you leave his name off the birth

certificate," he said. "After all, he didn't even know about him."

And the man was dead, right? What harm could possibly come from keeping his identity a secret? Their own late father had been a good-for-nothing cheat who also suffered from addiction, and had been all too happy to let Justin work odd jobs to keep a roof over the family's head. Sadie's newborn child needed to be— *deserved to be*—protected, cared for and sheltered from his family's problems, in a way that Justin never was.

The baby fussed softly, but not like he was upset. More like he was new to having a voice and trying to figure out how to use it. Justin looked down at his nephew. His eyes were open and blue like Justin's and Sadie's.

"Have you decided on a name for him yet?" Justin asked.

"Not yet," Sadie said. "I still can't really believe that he's real."

"I get that." Justin's eyes were still on his nephew. "There are a lot of great names in the world and plenty of time to decide."

The baby looked at his new uncle thoughtfully.

"But there's something else." Sadie took a deep breath, as if summoning her courage. "I want you and Violet to adopt him."

"What?" Justin turned back, his breath leaving his lungs in a sudden rush.

Him parent this precious child? Raise him as his own?

Lord, You know how much I want to be a father. But I'm not ready. This kid deserves better than what I can give him.

"You're such a great person, and that one time I met your fiancée she seemed so nice."

"Violet and I broke up. Months ago. We called it off a few days before the wedding back in May."

He'd called it off. He'd been the one to break her heart.

Corporal Violet Jones of the RCMP's Missing Persons Unit was the most beautiful and extraordinary person he'd ever met. Somehow Justin had convinced her to marry him. And then he'd bailed, like a coward, less than a week before the wedding, because he'd been overwhelmed. There'd been major chaos on his new team at work and multiple crises within his extended family. He'd been running around like a chicken with its head cut off, trying to put out too many fires at once—as mixed as that metaphor might be—and realized he had no right to bring a woman as extraordinary as Violet into his mess.

Or the kids they'd both wanted to have.

"It's okay if you forgot. You've been going through a lot. And I'm really, incredibly flattered that you want me to adopt your baby, but—"

"Don't keep saying it's okay!" Sadie cut him off. Did he? Her voice was pleading. "You're always saying things are okay when they're not. I can't take care of him. I'm not ready to be a mom. But you'll be an amazing dad. I just know you will. You're the best person I know. You're so good at taking care of everyone, all the time. I know you'll teach him how to tie his shoes and ride a bike and—"

"Hey." Justin laid a gentle hand on his sister's arm. "You just caught me by surprise. But I'll think about it.

I promise. And no matter what happens I'm going to do my best to take care of both him and you. All right?"

Sadie nodded, but he could tell by the way the light dimmed in her eyes that she was worried about what his answer would be.

"Now I need to get back to work." Not to mention take some time to think and pray about the bombshell his half sister had just dropped in his lap. "But I'll pop in later tonight and see you both then. I promise."

He gave her what he hoped was a reassuring smile. She gave him a watery one in return, then she leaned her head back against the pillows and closed her eyes. Justin looked down at his nephew. The baby had fallen asleep. Justin ran his finger down the infant's soft cheek. Then he stepped out into the hallway and closed the door behind him.

He'd made it all the way down to the end of the maternity floor hallway when an elderly nurse with a clipboard stopped him.

"Are you Miss Sadie Roach's social worker?"

"No. I'm family."

The nurse frowned. "She has no family listed on file."

"It's complicated."

His mother refused to acknowledge his illegitimate half sister's existence. There was no legal record he and Sadie were related, and the fact Justin had stepped up and done his best to be Sadie's big brother had caused even more tension in their already splintered family. His mother was constantly in crisis. His brother was in and out of rehab. He couldn't imagine how they'd react if he adopted Sadie's son.

"Well, you might want to advise her to call her lawyer," the nurse said. "She was asking for drugs when she first came in and didn't even seem to realize she was in labor. Social services are planning on making a wellness check before she's released."

He listened and nodded as the nurse explained that hospitals had an obligation to contact social services when parents came in exhibiting certain symptoms. None of it was a surprise. Until recently social workers were even allowed to show up in the delivery room and take children from mothers like Sadie immediately, without even giving them an opportunity to bond with them. In some places, they still were. He glanced past the nurse and watched as a wiry male nurse in scrubs, with dark curly hair and an indent at the bridge of his nose, wheeled his nephew out of Sadie's room. He'd barely left her five minutes ago and already someone was taking the baby to the nursery.

"Thank you," Justin told the nurse with the clipboard. "I appreciate all this."

Justin continued down the hallway. His footsteps felt even heavier than before. A small family stood waiting for the elevator, so he took the stairs. It was the first week of January, but remnants of holiday decorations still lingered on office doors and hung from the ceiling.

Justin found himself heading for the chapel. Silence fell as he pushed through the large wooden doors, and they swung shut behind him. He slid into the back row. Stained glass windows—with brightly colored depictions of flying rain, flowers, wheat sheaths and snow, representing the four seasons—surrounded him.

He dropped to his knees and closed his eyes.

Help me, Lord. What do I do?

Unexpectedly, a question his youth pastor had asked him once, half a lifetime ago, filled his mind: "What do *you* want to do, Justin?"

What *did* he want to do?

Justin didn't have a good answer to that question. The person manning the lifeboat didn't get to chart a course or choose what direction he was headed. Yes, he'd wanted to be a father just as strongly as he'd wanted to be a husband. When Violet's doctor had advised them that due to medical complications it might take some time for her to get pregnant, they'd agreed to start trying for a family as soon as they got married and also look into adoption.

But a child deserved better than a dad like Justin who kept hopping out of bed at three in the morning to take his brother to rehab or look for his sister when she wandered out of a halfway house, especially after Justin had already taken on a double shift in the National Cybercrime Unit to cover for one colleague or another who needed a hand. Violet had deserved better from a husband, too.

Sadie had told him he was good at taking care of everyone. But she was wrong. Truth was, he thought he was pretty lousy at it. But he couldn't exactly let himself stop and think about the kind of life he wanted to have when people around him were drowning.

Suddenly, a siren pierced the stillness. It was high-pitched and unrelenting. Justin leaped to his feet. It was what they called a Code Amber—the specific alert they used when a child had been kidnapped from the premises. The hospital was going into lockdown.

He pushed through the door and ran down the hall, back toward the staircase that would lead him to his sister's floor, only to be blocked by a towering security guard in a dark blue uniform as he reached the main lobby. At five foot eight, Justin was used to most men being taller than he was. But this guard was like a mountain.

"I'm sorry, sir," the guard said. "Everyone's staying put for now."

"But I'm a police officer," Justin protested.

The guard's eyebrow rose. "Can I see some ID?"

Justin shook his head. He didn't carry his badge with him when he wasn't on duty, and the rules around child abductions were so strict he knew the guard wouldn't be authorized to make an exception. There'd been a spate of newborn abductions from hospitals across the country in recent months. None in British Columbia, but six weeks ago a child had been snatched from across the border in Alberta. Rumor within the RCMP Major Crimes Unit, which both Justin and Violet's departments fell under, was that some foreign criminal organization—called the L.B. Syndicate—was stealing newborns from vulnerable parents and then selling them off to wealthy couples.

Why had he left Sadie's side? What if something happened to his nephew?

Agonizing minutes ticked by, leaving him stuck behind the makeshift security checkpoint, waiting and praying as an uneasy stillness filled the empty hospital hallways, punctuated by frantic bursts of activity. Then double doors swung open at the end of the lobby, and a flurry of both uniformed and ununiformed officers he recognized from the Missing Persons Unit rushed through.

But he only had eyes for one—Corporal Violet Jones. She wore a crisp black blazer over a white blouse, with her bright gold badge hanging on a lanyard. Her gait was steady. Steely focus filled her gaze. Then her remarkable indigo eyes met his through rectangular glasses, and she faltered a step.

"Justin! What are you doing here?"

It was the first words she'd said to him since the day he'd called off their engagement.

"Sadie just had a baby."

Her eyes widened. Then a deep sadness washed over her features. Fear clutched his heart.

She nodded to the guard in front of him. "Let him through."

"Thank you," Justin called. But she'd already disappeared through another door. He bolted up the stairs to the maternity ward. But it was too late. Uniformed police officers had gathered around the door to Sadie's room. Her heartbreaking cries echoed down the hall.

His newborn baby nephew had been kidnapped.

The early morning world was cold, damp and gray as Violet stepped out a side door of the RCMP headquarters in Vancouver and jogged down the sidewalk in the hopes of finding her favorite coffee shop open. A dull ache sat heavy in her chest. The mood in the Missing Persons Unit was tense. It had been two and a half weeks since Justin's nephew had been snatched, just the latest in a string of six similar kidnappings across the country. Each one had been from a poor mother, with addiction and homelessness problems, no family, no money and no father listed on the birth certificate. The exact kind of person society tended not to care about.

But Sadie's child had been different. He'd had Justin. Sadie had checked out of the hospital and disappeared back into the seedier side of the streets, within hours of her baby's disappearance. Most of the mothers of the kidnapped babies had, maybe due to fear of involving police in their lives or the belief that no one would think they were worth helping. But Violet's former fiancé had been relentlessly pursuing the case. Justin had called her team six times in the past twenty-four hours alone. Her colleagues had followed up with him, but apparently whatever Justin's theory was none of them thought it held any water. And now it was only a matter of time before another child was ripped from their mother's arms.

Violet's boots trudged through ankle-deep slush. It was eight thirty on a Thursday, and storefronts to her left and right were closed. The city's snowplows hadn't cleared the streets and sidewalks yet. The sky had dumped almost two fresh feet of snow the night before, where it had quickly mixed with the dirty gray sludge and ice left over from the last snowfall.

Her eyes rose to the majestic Rocky Mountains that crested high above the town. Winter in the city could be an ugly business, but it sure was pretty in the mountains.

Lord, I'm looking for two different targets, she prayed, silently and methodically turning her case over to God. *The sellers aka the L.B. Syndicate who steal and traffic newborns. And the parents who buy the babies from them. You know who they are. Please, help me find a lead. Some tiny crack in their enterprise to wedge my foot in, and then from there take the entire operation down.*

She reached the coffee shop she'd been aiming for. A light was on inside, but the blinds were down, the door was locked and the sign read Closed. A figure in a red plaid jacket and a clashing blue-and-green Canucks toque stepped out of the alley. Instinctively, she braced herself to strike.

"Violet!" Justin's hands rose defensively. "Hey! It's okay. It's just me!"

"Justin. Hi."

She rocked back on her heels and lowered her hands.

"Sorry to startle you." His kind blue eyes, filled with an urgent, almost desperate look, met hers under the brim of his wool hat. "I need to talk to you about something, and I thought you'd be more comfortable if we did it over coffee, outside of headquarters, instead of the total goldfish bowl that the unit can be."

He wasn't wrong. Both she and Justin worked on separate floors of the same RCMP building. The gossip that swirled around after their wedding was called off had been worse than high school.

"Sadly, this place is closed."

"I know, but it's your favorite, so I talked to the owner, and she agreed to open it up for us."

That was Justin in a nutshell. "Preemptively caring," as she'd described it to her brother Anthony and his wife, Tessa, once. Justin had been the kind of romantic partner who'd never asked what she'd wanted. Instead, he'd figured it out and then just gone ahead and made it happen. Maybe she'd liked it at first. Even found it loving. Until she'd realized just how one-sided the whole thing was. Because he'd never let her take care of him in return. He'd never asked her for help. He'd never opened up about what he needed. Instead, he'd just bottled all his own worries up and acted like it was his job to make her happy. All the while she'd watched him get more and more weighed down and crushed by whatever secret burdens he was carrying that he wasn't willing to share.

Until he'd crumbled, taking their entire relationship with it.

"I know you've been talking to other people in my unit. I'm sure if there's any merit to your theories they'll pass it on to me."

"Violet, I think I've found my nephew, and I've figured out who his buyers are. They're going to leave the country in less than a week, and I need your unit to authorize an undercover rescue mission."

He pulled out his phone and held it up to show her a picture of a two-week-old baby in a blue blanket. It definitely looked like his nephew. But so had hundreds of other pictures sent in by members of the public that turned out to be nothing.

"I'm not the one you need to convince," she started.

Chief Superintendent Wade Zablocie of the Major

Crimes Unit was the one who had to sign off on opening an investigation into any specific family.

"I've tried every other officer in your unit. Not one has been willing to go to bat with Zablocie on this. Just give me ten minutes. Please, Violet. I need your help to rescue him before it's too late."

Something painful turned in her heart. This man had been her best friend, her favorite person and the one she thought she was going to spend the rest of her life with. But she couldn't remember Justin ever asking her for help before. Let alone pleading.

"Okay. Ten minutes."

They walked through a side door into the kitchen at the back of the coffee shop. A woman in her late fifties whom Violet knew by sight but not by name nodded and smiled to them as they passed. The place was empty except for a thin man with a hoodie pulled over his head, who was hunched over a laptop by the window. He looked familiar.

"Violet, meet Seth." Justin nodded to the man who raised a hand in greeting and then went back to his laptop. "He's arguably the country's best good-guy hacker, and he consults for the cybercrimes unit, specifically on the lengths that the L.B. Syndicate seller is willing to take to stop anyone from ever figuring out who's buying the children they're selling."

"So you're up to speed on the seller and buyer dynamic we've uncovered." Violet pulled off her glasses, cleaned them with a dry corner of her scarf and slid them back on.

"Yeah," Justin said. "I've put a chart up in the cybercrimes unit. It looks like the sun or a virus molecule. We've got L.B., who's trafficking kids, in the center and then the six unknown buyers jutting out the sides. We've been able to trace some payments on dark websites, but the details are always wiped before we can trace either the seller or buyers."

Yes, she knew all this through her own work within the RCMP. But it was good to know Justin was on the same page. Justin waved Violet toward the table for two in the opposite corner of the room, where she noted their coffee was already waiting. She sat down and so did he.

So Justin thought he'd found one of the buyers. Then why wasn't an undercover operation already underway?

"I also know the working theory is that the L.B. Syndicate has been going at it incredibly hard to stop anyone from uncovering them or their buyers," Justin said. "To the point that they're actively monitoring the web twenty-four seven to make sure nothing that exposes any of the buyers ever appears online."

"Yes, we believe the buyers are paying for security from L.B., not just a baby." Violet leaned her elbows on the table. "Although it's possible this so-called security is more of a threat to keep them silent."

"You know how I told you I found a recent picture of my nephew at two weeks old online?"

"Yes, but you haven't explained how or where yet." And he'd better get to it.

"Well, the picture was wiped from the internet within moments of someone posting it, and, fascinatingly, whenever I've tried posting that exact same picture anywhere online since, whatever website I use gets taken down within an instant, and my network's been hit with an online attack."

"And you think L.B. Syndicate's sellers are behind it?" she asked.

"Absolutely. So I've asked Seth to post a copy of that same two-week-old baby online right now, in front of you, using a private server he's rigged up. Then you can see for yourself in real time as someone attacks his domain and takes it down."

Which would indeed bolster his case that this kid he wanted to investigate really was his nephew. Justin was backstopping his claim, before she even took it to Zablocie with tangible proof. It was smart. And exactly the kind of thing she'd expect Justin to do.

"We don't want to use the RCMP system," Seth called from the far side of the room. He leaned back and cracked his knuckles. "Not just because they could create a whole mess in the system, but also because we don't want them realizing we're on to them. I'm going to be a little bit sloppy in covering my tracks, so hopefully they'll catch on to us quick. Then I'll record every keystroke they try to hit us with, which will hopefully help us figure out where it's coming from."

The hacker grinned and went back to his laptop.

Violet unzipped her jacket. The truth was her unit didn't have any solid leads as to who was behind the kidnappings. If Justin had found his nephew, located the person who'd bought him and managed to lure the L.B. Syndicate into attacking Seth's laptop, she'd have her first real shot at finding all the missing children and taking the traffickers down for good.

"Enough stalling," she said. "Let's get to who bought your nephew, where he is now and how you found his picture."

Justin blinked. "I wasn't stalling. I was just trying to lay everything out in the right order."

His order, in other words. Justin unwrapped his scarf and pulled off his hat. Dark rings lined his blue eyes. His blond hair was shaggy, and the stubble that lined his jaw told her that he hadn't shaved in days. He took a deep breath and started.

"Ever since Sadie's baby was kidnapped, I've had an online search running, twenty-four hours a day, for any sign of him. Anytime, day or night, an alarm goes off so I don't miss a possible sighting, no matter how remote."

No wonder he looked like he hadn't slept in weeks.

"You must've gotten hundreds of false alarms."

"Thousands. A little over forty-eight hours ago, an eighty-two-year-old woman in Eastern Europe posted this picture of her great-grandnephew to a closed seniors' chat group. She didn't realize anyone outside her retirement building could see it."

"Obscure place to find a lead in a Canadian kidnapping case," Violet said.

"The picture disappeared off the site less than ten minutes later, replaced by a very tearful apology saying her grandniece Emelia didn't want any pictures of the baby posted anywhere for privacy reasons."

"Which isn't necessarily unusual," Violet pointed out. "A lot of new parents don't want their kids' pictures online."

"Less than twenty-four hours later, this great-aunt

was dead. Apparent natural causes, nothing obviously suspicious, but the coroner did note high levels of sleeping pills in her system."

Violet whistled.

"Now, that's a pretty big coincidence." And maybe a sign of just how far this seller syndicate was willing to go to stop any glimmer of information about their operation getting out. "I take it you've located Emelia?"

"I have. Took a lot of online digging, but I found her. Emelia DuBois has been married to Francois DuBois for three years. He goes by Frank. Unhappy marriage based on what we've been able to find of Frank's social media philandering. They're from Eastern Europe, living at a very remote wilderness camp in the Rockies. They call my nephew Matty—short for Matthias—and say it was a home birth. They're scheduled to move to Scandinavia a week from now to be closer to their extended family."

"And you're worried that once they leave the country with him it'll be hard to get an extradition treaty since we won't have jurisdiction."

"Yup, so the clock is ticking."

She leaned forward.

"What do we know about the camp?"

"It's called the Mount Prince Wilderness Resort. She was a receptionist, and he was their main sports instructor. It's extremely remote and hard to get to. There's only one way in and out, and the road's so treacherous visitors have to park at the base of Mount Prince and get one of the camp's three all-terrain vehicles to drive them up. Right now, it's closed for the season and has less than ten full-time staff living on-site. It's also financially struggling. The owner is hosting some potential investors from other wilderness camps this weekend to see if one or more will bail them out, and I've got an in that we can use to infiltrate that."

Both Violet and Justin had spent a lot of time at similar places, hiking through the woods and rappelling down cliffs. It was not the kind of place she'd expect to find criminals who'd bought somebody else's stolen baby.

"And it's an unhappy marriage?"

"It looks like they were heading for divorce before Emelia 'got pregnant.'" Justin's fingers put air quotes around the last two words. "She's got health problems of some kind, but I don't know what they are. She's posted a lot online about her pregnancy over the past nine months, and apparently it was a rough one. She was sick a lot. Frank was away overseas visiting family for the last trimester and most of the second as well, leaving her to handle it on her own. So it's quite possible he had no idea she wasn't actually pregnant. He only came back when Matty arrived. It was a 'home birth.' The baby was 'delivered' by the camp's nurse practitioner, Ariel Fallis, while Frank was out of the country. Ariel's the one who filed the official 'notice of birth' with the government. She's now been hired as their nanny and is flying overseas with them."

Violet pushed her glasses up higher on the bridge of her nose. A picture was forming in her mind.

"So the theory is we've got a woman who fakes being pregnant to keep her wayward husband from leaving her. The question is how did she turn to a kidnapping ring? And how did she talk her friend into helping her?"

"I don't know," Justin admitted.

"Was Frank in on it? I can't see why he'd ever go along with it, especially if their marriage was already on the rocks. And is the fact they're moving overseas just a fortunate coincidence or part of the plan?"

"Again, I don't know." Justin's brow furrowed, and the lines between his eyes deepened.

"Why do I get the feeling the other shoe's about to drop?"

Justin shifted uncomfortably in his seat.

"Frank's grandmother runs the world's fourth largest energy company. She's quite elderly, and apparently succession plans are underway to pass the company on to Frank's uncle when she dies. She has lots of friends among Canadian politicians and law enforcement. Our government is currently negotiating with them to help on our upcoming pipeline."

Violet sucked in a breath.

"You do realize how big a public relations nightmare it will be for the RCMP if we accuse a member of a powerful foreign family of kidnapping a baby and we're wrong? The potential blowback could sink both our careers. Maybe even ding Zablocie's."

"That's why I need you to help me prove that Matty is my nephew before it's too late." He reached across the table, and his fingers enveloped hers.

"Hey, guys?" Seth's worried voice came from the other side of the room. "Don't want to alarm anyone, but I think the L.B. Syndicate has tracked our address."

"You mean your computer's IP address, right?" Justin asked.

The hacker shook his head.

"No." Seth's face paled. "Our physical address. Here. This coffee shop."

Justin stood. Violet did, too.

"I'm sorry," Seth said. "They've had it for about ten minutes, but I only caught it now."

"But they're not based here," Violet started.

Then again, they'd kidnapped and sold a baby here recently. Maybe they'd left an operative behind to make sure the sale went well.

Suddenly a black van pulled up outside on the slushy road. The back door rolled open.

"Get down!" she shouted.

Gunfire sounded.

Justin threw his body over hers and pulled her to the ground, as the coffee shop window exploded in a spray of glass.

TWO

Sometimes seconds stretched out until they felt like an eternity, Justin thought as he lay on the cold tile floor with Violet pressed against his chest and broken glass raining down around them.

Then, just as suddenly as the gunfire had started, it was all over. He heard the sound of the van peeling away.

Violet rolled out of his arms. She leaped to her feet, as did he.

"Everyone all right?" she shouted.

As Justin called simultaneously, "Is everyone okay?"

"I'm okay." Seth was crouched under a table. "But my laptop has seen better days. I thought you said this L.B. Syndicate was based overseas."

"I'm guessing they have someone local, too," Violet said. "Maybe when a baby is trafficked they dispatch someone to keep an eye on the buyer to make sure nothing goes wrong."

Snow blew through the hole where the window had been and sent the twisted remains of the blinds dancing. Violet yanked her phone from her pocket, dialed a number and held it to her ear as she ran for the kitchen.

From what he could hear, it sounded like she was on the phone with RCMP dispatch. He turned back to Seth as the hacker climbed to his feet. His laptop had been reduced to fragments of plastic and metal that now littered the floor.

Violet rushed back into the room.

"Two civilians in the back," she said. "Both are fine. The owner of the café has already gotten through to 911. Local police are on their way."

Justin's heart ached for the kind business owner who'd agreed to open the place for them.

Police sirens wailed in the distance.

"Seth, do you think the people behind this know who we are?" Violet asked. "Did they see our faces? Could they identify us?"

"I don't think so," Seth said. "For my part, I was on an anonymous server."

"Plus, you and I were sitting in the back of the room," Justin added, "and the blinds were drawn. Why?"

He watched as relief rolled off Violet's shoulders.

"Okay. Then I say we let local police be the face of this, and all RCMP involvement stays below the radar."

"Why?" Justin asked.

Determination shone in her indigo eyes.

"Because I'm going to tell Zablocie we want a meeting in his office within the hour. I still don't know if your theory is correct. But we're clearly up against a pretty powerful enemy with incredible reach. Justin, you're one of the most cautious people I know. You've convinced me you're on to something, and if there's even a possibility that whoever just shot at us is connected to the baby kidnapping ring, I'm willing to put my neck on the line to find out."

It ended up being closer to two hours before Justin and Violet stood before Zablocie and Justin made his case. He had stayed behind at the coffee shop to help the owners sweep up the floor and nail boards over the windows, once local police had cleared them to tidy up the scene. Meanwhile, Violet had started the ball rolling with Zablocie.

Now Justin's nerves rattled like loose change as they stood before Zablocie's desk. The chief superintendent was an imposing man with a square jaw and the kind of white, bushy mustache that reminded Justin of every chief who pounded a desk and shouted in a 1980s cartoon. Not that he'd ever heard Zablocie so much as raise his voice. He didn't need to. The man was intimidating enough without it. Two goldfishes, one black and one orange, swam in lazy circles around a bowl behind his desk. He'd heard they were gifts from Zablocie's granddaughter.

Violet stood back and let Justin do the talking. He couldn't help but notice that she'd freshened up a bit since the incident back at the coffee shop. Even in a simple blazer and slacks and with minimal makeup on, she was a knockout. While Justin was still finding bits of glass stuck to his clothes and his hair still looked like he'd been dragged through some bushes on his way to the meeting, even after his best attempt to smooth it down.

"Despite what you both seem to think," Zablocie said,

"I did have someone look into this potential lead regarding the DuBois family after Justin raised it to other members of the team. Law enforcement ruled the great-aunt's death was an accident. And as for the shooting that just happened at the coffee shop, local police have already caught and arrested the shooters. They're members of a local gang and claim they got a faulty tip that it was the location of a rival gang's stash house. You guys were just in the wrong place at the wrong time."

Violet snorted. She seemed far less cowed by the boss than Justin felt. "Let me guess. The text was from an encrypted and untraceable number?"

"It was," Zablocie conceded.

"And how do you explain the fact Justin and Seth suffered a cyberattack whenever they tried to do a reverse image search of two-week-old Matty's picture?" she pressed.

"The DuBois family is very wealthy and powerful. They aren't above hiring a black-market cybersecurity team to keep unwanted things about family members off the internet." Zablocie leaned back and his chair squeaked. "Truth is, there's not a single part of your theory that's so ironclad that I can't knock it down. And that's a problem for us. Frank's grandmother is friends with people way above my pay grade. Custody cases are notoriously difficult, and if something goes wrong with the investigation, all of us could jeopardize our careers."

Justin's heart sank. But as he watched, Violet's chin rose.

"You said *us*." She leaned forward and rested her palms on the table. "Which tells me you don't want to drop this anymore than we do. I can understand why this department would be hesitant to authorize an investigation against a powerful foreign family without nailing down the evidence. But six babies have been snatched in the past few months. This syndicate is ruthless. Justin is bringing us a solid lead about one of the buyers. We've strategically kept the fact Sadie has a half brother out of the media, so Justin's identity hasn't been compromised. And considering the fact the DuBois couple will be leaving the country in the next few days, I'd rather launch an investigation into them and get it wrong than let someone who bought a stolen baby slip through our fingers."

Zablocie closed his eyes and blew out a long breath. Then he opened them again. "What's your plan? You said they're currently in some very remote cabin in the Rockies. I assume you've got a way in?"

"Yes," Justin said. "But we need to move fast. The camp's in financial trouble. The owner, Ross Halton, is looking for investors. He's invited some couples from other camps and wilderness adventure outfits across Canada to visit this weekend so he can razzle-dazzle them into giving him money. I'm friends with Quinn Dukes-Cooper who runs Dukes Wilderness Adventures. Her husband, Jeff, is with the Canadian Rangers and her brother-in-law is a former undercover detective. They're good people. Some of the best. Both Violet and I are very experienced wilderness campers, and they've offered to let us go in undercover as representatives of their camp. We'd be Josh Cooper, Jeff's imaginary cousin, and his wife, Viv."

Violet blinked. Yeah, he hadn't told her that part.

"But of course, we're under no obligation to go with this plan if you can come up with a better one," Justin said, quickly. "Or if it's easier for everyone, I can just tackle it alone."

"No. If we're doing this, you're taking Corporal Jones with you. This is her department's investigation." Zablocie turned to Violet. "What do you say? It's your call."

Violet pressed her lips together. A long silence spread across the room until Justin thought the air itself would shatter from the tension.

"I say we do it," Violet said. "We go in, we find something with the baby's DNA on it that we can test against Sadie to prove the kid is hers and we get out again, as quickly as possible. Then we regroup and strategize our next steps from there. Twenty-four hours tops. Hopefully less."

"Very good." Zablocie leaned back in his chair. "I want to see your plan on my desk by the end of the day."

The meeting ended, and both Justin and Violet left the office and entered the hall. He turned to head back toward his unit.

"One second."

He looked back. "Justin, before we embark on this mission, I need to ask you something important, and it's essential that you tell me the truth."

"Okay."

"Is there any possibility that something else is going on here? Something that has nothing to do with this L.B. Syndicate who's been kidnapping babies and selling them. Am I right in believing that you haven't had any contact with Sadie since she checked herself out of hospital? And that the story is true that the baby's father is presumed dead and never even knew she was pregnant with his child?"

Justin's promise to his sister back in the hospital room filled his mind.

"The truth is that I haven't seen Sadie since the day her son was kidnapped. She checked out of the hospital and disappeared onto the streets. She doesn't want to be found." If she's even still alive. "Sadie gave me her word that my nephew's father was a criminal who died before he even knew she was pregnant, and I believe her."

Her eyes searched his face for a long moment.

"I get why Major Crimes made the call to keep the fact this baby's mother's half brother was an RCMP officer out of the news, and I'm really glad we did. But the fact of the matter is this L.B. Syndicate case is different. These kids are different, and their families are different. At least in some people's eyes. I know our motto in the RCMP is *Maintiens le Droit*—uphold what's right. Regardless of who the victim and criminal are. But I'm not going to pretend that there won't be some among Zablocie's superiors who'll be a little hesitant to arrest a man like Frank DuBois, with all his family's wealth and connections, in order to return the child to a woman like Sadie."

Justin rocked back on his heels. "You don't want to do it."

"Of course, I want to do it, and I will. Because it's the right thing to do. I just want to make sure that you know the stakes. It's not only your career on the line if we mess this up. It's mine and maybe even Zablocie's, too."

"I know." It was ironic. Justin had called off the wedding to spare Violet from the chaos of his family and life. Now here he was, asking her to put her career on the line for him. "Just like I know I didn't have the right to ask you for anything after what happened between us, and I'm really grateful you went to bat for me in there like that."

But despite the warmth of gratitude welling up in his core, her gaze was as cold as steel.

"Let me be clear. I didn't do it for you. I did it for your nephew, for the five other kids who've been kidnapped, their families and for whatever poor mother and child the L.B. Syndicate is targeting next. No matter what kind of family situation they were born into, they deserve better than to be treated like objects. I'm going to do whatever it takes to stop the people doing this to them. Even if I have to put my career on the line in the process. I only wanted to double-check we were on the same page and you weren't going to let me down."

Then, before he could say anything more, she turned and walked down the hallway without looking back.

The late-morning sun glistened off the snow-covered Rocky Mountains, making the trees and cliffs outside the truck's windows dazzle and shine like diamonds. Violet sat in the passenger seat of an RCMP undercover assignment pickup truck that reminded her far too much of the one Justin used to drive back when they were dating. Justin was behind the wheel.

To her surprise, before Justin had picked her up that morning he'd dropped by the very same café where they'd been shot at the day before and bought them both coffees and bagels. Apparently, he'd gone over there after work last night and helped them install a new front window, patch up the walls and repaint, so they'd be able to reopen this morning without missing a day of business.

It was a three-hour drive from Vancouver to the base of Mount Prince in the Rockies. There they'd park their truck, and a staff vehicle would pick them up to take them up the steep and inhospitable road to the camp. The truck had been given a bit of a makeover, with old-looking new license plates and a fresh registration number, both of which were registered to Josh Cooper. Bumper stickers advertised Dukes Wilderness Adventures, the importance of protecting the wetlands and braking for turtles. But inside the truck, the faint smell of coffee with milk and Justin's favorite brand of soap swirled around her, just as it had all those countless nights they'd sat in the flatbed of a similar truck, looked up at the stars and planned out their lives together.

Violet's eyes had never tolerated contacts. So she'd switched her usual glasses for ones with tinted lenses that dulled her distinctive indigo irises to look a dull gray. Hair extensions stretched her black hair from a chin-length bob down to the middle of her back. Justin had tidied his beard, darkened his hair and switched his usual shaggier locks for a crisp and rather handsome crewcut. Lifts hidden in his winter boots had added an extra inch and a half to his height. If kidnappers had spotted a scruffy-looking man visiting Sadie in her hospital room, Justin looked nothing like that now.

The day before, she'd hurried back to her office as soon as the meeting with Zablocie was over, wanting to put as much distance as possible between them, and to figure out how she was going to settle her mind for the mission ahead. But now it was just her and Justin, alone and relying on each other until they got the DNA evidence they needed to prove Matty DuBois was really Sadie's son.

Her eyes closed and she prayed.

Lord, help me and guide me. Keep my mind clear from distraction.

She was officially the one heading this undercover mission, with Justin on board as a consulting officer. Missing Persons was her unit, and the missing babies were her primary focus, while Justin had a personal connection to the case. Technically she outranked him in seniority, too, having joined the RCMP two years before Justin had, although that had never been an issue in their relationship as far as she was concerned, because they were in separate departments.

Violet could honestly say she felt confident about putting her own reputation on the line for this mission. She was absolutely certain she'd asked the right questions, raised the correct concerns, made the absolute best call and hadn't let any of her personal feelings get in the way. So far.

Her brother, best friend and childhood rival—RCMP Sergeant Anthony Jones of the Major Crimes Unit—

had volunteered to be their handler and main contact with the outside world. One of the tricks to a successful undercover mission was keeping the fake identity as close to the real one when possible and it had been decided that he'd pose as Viv's brother, too. Zablocie had wanted to keep the circle of knowledge about the operation as small as possible. Mostly to avoid the risk of leaks but also because they couldn't be completely sure that somebody, somewhere up in the RCMP ranks, wasn't in the pockets of DuBois Oil and Gas. Whenever Frank's grandma was in Canada she had a habit of throwing fundraising galas for local charities, and top law enforcement brass and politicians were frequently in attendance.

Not to mention Violet's brother Anthony was an excellent officer.

But having him on the case still reminded her that when she'd been fourteen, Anthony had told that her she coasted through life because she was pretty. He'd apologized for it since, several times over. Yet the comment had stuck with her, like a splinter buried under her skin, and ever since then she'd felt driven to prove herself, achieve excellence and make sure every single one of her accomplishments could stand on its own merits. It had left her feeling like she was always just one botched mission away from losing the reputation she'd striven to build. And considering how high the stakes were for the mission, and her personal history with Justin, this case was more perilous than most.

Already it felt like every molecule of her body was too attuned to Justin's gestures and movements. His crinkled forehead told her that he was worried. His fingers drumming on the steering wheel meant he was trying to distract himself by playing some unheard music in his head.

"I'm hoping we can wrap this whole thing up in less than a day. I know we're scheduled to be there two nights. But there's no reason to stay there any longer than we have to."

Justin nodded. "Absolutely."

"Our mission is simple. We get a sample of Matty's DNA, rush it to the lab and have it tested to prove he's your nephew. Without a warrant, that means collecting something he's left his DNA on, like a bottle or blanket. We should also make sure you get eyes on Matty, so we have your personal verification as a witness and if possible get a good, clear picture of him we can put out to international police if they try to disappear."

Justin hesitated as if he was debating what to say. "Copy that."

She glanced at him sideways. Did she sound too formal about all this? Too official? Too direct? They were colleagues now. Nothing more. He had to know that. He was the one who hadn't wanted to marry her. She'd wanted a future together, but he'd slammed that door in her face, and she wasn't about to go knocking on it now.

"My biggest concern is how we even get access to Matty," she started. Then she caught herself and stopped. "I'm sorry, I just realized I keep calling him by the name his buyers gave him. Within our team we just call him baby number six, in the order he was stolen, and he was snatched before Sadie completed his birth certificate. What should I call him?"

"Calling him Matty is fine. She hadn't officially decided on a name yet. And yeah, I'm concerned about how we're going to get access to the baby, too. By the sound of things, Ross, the owner, has our whole time up there pretty tightly planned out with his sales pitch. I don't know how easy it will be for us to slip away from that."

The road curved upward as they drove deeper and deeper into the Rocky Mountains. Justin pulled off the road into a smaller rural highway that was made even narrower by the fallen snow.

"Plus, if the L.B. Syndicate did kidnap my nephew to sell to the DuBois family," Justin went on, "they might have one of their operatives up there this weekend keeping an eye on things. The person I saw rolling the baby out of the nursery definitely wasn't Frank DuBois."

Despite security footage of the man and a police sketch, he still hadn't been identified.

"My team calls him Curly, for want of a better name. As far as people at the camp are concerned, we have three targets." She ticked the suspects off on her fingers. "Emelia, who we believed faked her pregnancy. Ariel, the nurse and nanny who helped her cover it up. And Frank, who may or may not have been aware of what was going on. I'm assuming Frank is a secondary victim in all this, considering he wasn't even in the country when Matty was supposedly born, and he missed most of the pregnancy. But I may be wrong."

Justin nodded. She leaned back against the seat.

"Ariel fascinates me the most," she went on. "Why help a friend fake a pregnancy if you've got nothing to gain from it? Why pretend to deliver a baby you didn't deliver? She's the one who filed the official form notifying the government that Matty had been born, which makes her guilty of fraud at the very least. Maybe even accessory to kidnapping after the fact. What did she have to gain from going along with this?"

"All good questions," Justin said.

A tall wooden archway announced they'd reached the Mount Prince Wilderness Resort parking lot. Justin pulled through and stopped the truck. There was about a dozen vehicles in the lot. Suddenly, a white all-terrain SUV appeared on their left, through a thick shock of trees that was so tight she hadn't even realized a road lay between them. A man in a bright green Mount Prince Wilderness Resort jacket leaped out. He was in his early thirties and stocky, with a dark beard and million-watt smile.

"Okay," Justin said, as if to himself, "Game time."

Violet whispered a prayer and then they got out of the truck.

"Hey, folks!" the man called with a cheerful wave. "I'm Lorenzo Segreto, chief of operations here at Mount Prince. You must be the Coopers from Duke Wilderness Adventures."

"We sure are. I'm Josh, and this is my wife, Viv."

"Nice to meet you." Lorenzo shook their hands.

"Are we late?" Violet asked. "Is everyone else already here?"

"No not at all," Lorenzo said. They walked around

to the back of the truck and grabbed their luggage and sleeping bags. "We spaced out your arrivals so we could take you up to the mountain one group at a time. We've got four groups total joining us this weekend. Two have arrived so far, and I'll be picking up the final one after I take you to your cabin. Then we'll all have a light lunch together in the main lodge, which will give you a chance to meet everyone."

"Sounds wonderful." Violet smiled.

They transferred their stuff to the back of Lorenzo's SUV, then Violet took the passenger seat and Justin sat in the back. The vehicle wasn't just all-wheel drive, she noted. It also had a manual transmission and heavy snow chains on the tires. The road up to the camp was incredibly steep and narrow. High cliffs rose on one side and plunged down cavernously on the other, until it felt like they were just inches away from tumbling straight down over the edge to their deaths. Mountaintops spread out above and beneath them in an endless array of white-capped pines. An eagle soared below them. Violet gasped.

Lorenzo turned to her. "Beautiful, isn't it?"

"It's stunning," she admitted. "I mean, I knew before we got here that the site was really remote and that there was only one way in and out. But seeing it firsthand…"

She blew out a long breath as her words trailed off.

Lorenzo chuckled. "Gives you a whole new perspective, doesn't it? I love this place. That's why it's so important to get folks like you up here to see for yourself what makes our camp so special."

Isolated and also dangerous.

"Is this road the only way in and out of the camp?" Justin leaned forward.

"We do have a network of hiking paths that run from the bottom of the ski hill gondolas all the way to the parking lot."

"How long is the hike?" Violet asked.

"About an hour and a half to walk down," Lorenzo said. "Three hours to walk up. But the paths are overgrown, and the ski lift has been out of commission for a couple of years now." An almost wistful look filled Lorenzo's eyes. "The potential of Mount Prince is incredible. We're only using a fraction of the grounds and facilities, but the repairs we need to get it up to scratch. are pretty extensive."

"And what do you do?" Violet asked.

"Everything." Lorenzo laughed. It was a warm, comfortable sound that seemed to fill the vehicle. "I run the camp on a day-to-day basis. I'm in charge of all the practical stuff. Ross is more of a big-picture guy. This is just one of several properties he owns, and he's not here that often."

They kept driving until the incline rose so steeply that Lorenzo had to downshift into third gear. The tops of buildings began to appear ahead of them through the trees. She spied the unused ski lift through the trees to her right and what looked like dilapidated cottages down an unpaved driveway to her left.

"Right now, we cater mostly to couples and small groups," Lorenzo went on. "Our standard cabins have two bunk beds and a couch in the living room. Sorry, we're not the kind of place that's set up for double beds, so I'm glad you remembered your sleeping bags. Electricity gets spotty when the weather's bad, so each cabin comes complete with a wood-burning stove. Our goal is to accommodate larger groups and younger kids. But that'll mean refurnishing our unused cabins and improving both the road and the electrical grid."

Violet checked her phone. The signal was dead. "What about cell service?"

"There are landlines in the main office, and we have our own small cell tower," Lorenzo said. "Internet and cell phone signals are patchy. They're strongest in the lodge and worse the farther you get from it. Good when the weather's great, and lousy when the wind is blowing."

Well, that was hardly comforting.

They rounded a corner, and suddenly a large wooden lodge loomed ahead of them. The building was nothing short of majestic, with towering front windows that reflected back the blue skies and green forest around them. It seemed to be constructed entirely of huge logs, each five or six feet thick. It wasn't until Lorenzo expertly drove them past the main entrance and around to the side that Violet saw the far more modest wing at the back that housed the kitchen. Lorenzo parked his vehicle in a small lot between a tall pile of firewood and rows of industrial garbage cans. Violet noted the two other camp SUVs were the only other vehicles in the lot. Then Lorenzo led them on foot through the site to their cabin, chatting amiably and pointing out smaller structures and facilities as they went.

The first thing that hit her was how truly isolated

they were. They were almost trapped, considering the only way out was to either take one of the vehicles behind the lodge or get someone to drive them back to their truck. The second thing she realized was just how misleading the online maps of the camp had been. They'd effectively flattened the site as if all the buildings were on the same level, when in reality the ground was so uneven they were constantly either walking up or downhill along narrow paths with no ability to see who or what might be lurking around the corner.

From a threat-assessment standpoint, this place was a nightmare.

"You said you have eight staff living up here year-round," she asked.

"Yup. Two couples. Four singles."

"Did I hear you're hiring?" Justin asked.

Lorenzo nodded. "One of the couples had a baby last month. They're moving at the end of the week, which is why Ross threw this impromptu investor weekend together quickly while we still had a nurse and athletics instructor on staff. My friend Ariel, the nurse, is going with the mom and dad as their nanny."

Then, for the first time since they'd met him, Lorenzo's omnipresent smile faded.

A series of small wooden cabins lay ahead. They were cropped together tightly, with only two or three trees separating them. Cabin number one and two had their lights on, and three was dark. Lorenzo led them to number four. He unlocked the door to their cabin with the kind of standard metal key that could easily be replaced by a bent paper clip or bobby pin. Then Lorenzo handed them a key attached to a small block of wood.

"What happens if we lose it?" Justin asked.

"Oh, don't worry," Lorenzo said, cheerfully. "The staff have master keys."

The cabin was dark and smelled of wood. Lorenzo leaned around the corner and hit a light switch. Dim yellow light flooded the room. The cabin was small, with an unevenly stuffed couch, wooden chair, a scratched coffee table and the wood-burning stove. There was a door at the back of the room, which she guessed led to the bedroom.

"Again, the electricity can be a bit hit-or-miss this time of year," Lorenzo said. "So I suggest you keep a flashlight handy and your woodstove ready to go."

Violet glanced at her cell phone. It had no bars. "You said the Wi-Fi is good in the lodge?"

"It's not actually good anywhere on-site. But it's usually the least terrible in the lodge. It comes and goes. There's a map on the table if you need help finding your way around. But we do ask that you don't leave the main area without a guide. The paths can get pretty treacherous."

Lorenzo wished them happy unpacking and told them a triangle would sound at the lodge when food was ready. He thanked them for coming, and Justin and Violet thanked him for the warm welcome. When he left, Justin turned to Violet.

"Are you thinking what I'm thinking?"

"That when we do get a sample of Matty's DNA it

won't exactly be that simple to just pop off back to Vancouver?"

"Yeah. Seeing the snow chains on top of snow tires, with a four-wheel-drive manual transmission, gave me pause about the road. Kinda feels like we're trapped here, doesn't it?"

Violet pulled off her boots and almost winced at how cold the floors were through her stocking feet. Justin knelt in front of the wood-burning stove and started to build a fire. She followed an odd garlicky smell to the corner of the room and found a rodent trap filled with rat poison.

"We've got a rodent problem. And furniture that needs to be replaced."

"And this cabin is hardly secure," he added. "Thankfully, I've brought some simple but solid latch bolts I can attach to the back of the door to keep anyone from just letting themselves in while we're here, and a tiny security camera I can mount over the frame so we can see if anyone comes in when we're gone. Not to mention a complete set of baby supplies in case of emergency."

Violet resisted the urge to remind him their mission was to get Matty's DNA sample and get out. Nothing more. Zablocie had stressed before they left that they weren't authorized to remove Matty from the DuBois family unless his life was in immediate danger and it was the only way to save his life. She picked up their bags and walked through into the other room, leaving the third equipment bag behind. They'd take turns between sleeping in the bedroom and keeping watch in the living room. Two narrow bunk beds sat on opposite sides of the wall. A small window, closed with heavy wooden shutters, lay between them. She tossed her bag onto one of the bunks and Justin's on another.

Then she asked God for strength and wisdom. Lorenzo's welcome had been so warm. And yet a bitter cold seemed to sweep through the cabin like it was trying to burrow its way under her skin. Was there something wrong with this place? Or was it run by well-meaning people who'd been taken advantage of by a criminal?

Something cracked in the bushes outside. It sounded like footsteps. Her lips parted to call Justin, but she caught herself and closed them again for fear whoever was outside would hear her. Instead, she crept to the window, slid her finger between the slats, pried them open an inch and peered out.

She gasped as the police sketch she'd been looking at for two weeks seemed to come to life before her eyes. A man with dark curly hair and a crooked nose stood in the tree line. The same person who'd posed as a fake nurse and kidnapped Justin's nephew from the hospital was there, at the camp, and he was watching them.

THREE

Justin heard Violet gasp, as if she'd been about to scream and just barely managed to muffle the sound. He leaped to his feet and ran for the bedroom door, only to nearly crash headlong into Violet as she dashed back out into the living room.

"Are you okay?"

"I'm fine." Violet brushed passed him and sprinted to the front door. "There's someone outside watching our cabin." She shoved her feet into her boots. "I think it's 'Curly,' the same man who kidnapped your nephew from the hospital."

"Are you sure?" Justin rushed into the bedroom and opened the shutters. "He's not there now."

Violet didn't answer. He came back into the living room and found it empty. He pulled on his own boots and hurried outside. Violet was standing by the bedroom window, looking at the ground. As her eyes met his she raised a finger to her lips. He walked toward her, and as he reached her, she leaned her head close to his.

"He's gone," Violet whispered. Her hair brushed the side of his face. "It's hard to tell for sure which footprints are his, as they get a bit muddled with everyone else's prints when they hit the path. But it looks like he's been checking out the neighboring cabins as well. My guess is he's spying on everyone."

"And you're sure it's the same guy who kidnapped my nephew?"

"I can't know for certain. I never got a firsthand look at Curly and I'm pretty sure he didn't see me. According to the security footage we were able to glean he came up the back stairs, grabbed the baby and left. So, our paths never overlapped. But if it is the same guy, what does that mean? Does he work here? Has the syndicate sent him here to keep an eye on the DuBois family?"

"I don't know." But Justin was looking forward to finding out.

They went back into the cabin and spent a few minutes unpacking, then bundled up in their hats and scarves and slipped out for what was intended to look like a very casual stroll around the resort. Each of them hid plastic gloves, evidence bags and a simple lock-picking kit in deep pockets concealed inside their jackets.

The backup locks Justin had brought could unfortunately only be used to bar the door from the inside when they were there inside the cabin, but the security camera he'd hidden over the lintel would warn them if anyone broke in.

First they traced the footprints of the man Violet had seen watching their cabin until they lost them on the path. It definitely looked like he'd been spying on their neighbors as well. Then they wandered around the main areas of the site. They walked slowly, chatted lightly and said hello to the odd person they spotted, while they both got the lay of the land. Seemed all of the staff wore the same bright green jacket Lorenzo had.

A triangle sounded through the air.

Violet whispered, "Game time."

"Any advice for my first official undercover mission?" he whispered back.

"Stick as close to the truth as you can whenever possible. People distrust those they think are fake." She paused. "You're really great with people, Justin, and they tend to like you."

They made their way to the lodge, up the steps and through the door, where they left their coats on heavily laden pegs at the front of the room. About twenty people drifted around a room big enough to fit at least two hundred. A wide support pole stood in the center of the room, stretching from the floor to the ceiling rafters, forming an unofficial divider between the two sides of the room. The right seemed to be a dining area with folded tables and chairs stacked against the wall and a pass-through to the kitchen. The left side was more of a lounge area with overstuffed couches and a fireplace. He counted one potential exit to the left side of the room and a long hallway beside the kitchen pass-through, which he guessed led to a second.

A circle of chairs was set up in the dining area. Tables laden with platters of food dotted the room. The staff wore bright green fleece vests the same shade as their jackets. He didn't see Frank, Emelia or Matty anywhere. He couldn't see Ariel the nanny or Curly either.

He and Violet joined a small cluster of fellow potential investors in front of the fireplace, helped themselves to the rustic sandwiches that were laid out on a coffee table and joined in the conversation.

Toby and Carol Whitcher were the first couple to introduce themselves. The pair had short gray haircuts and matching blue plaid shirts with Bayfield Bible Camp embroidered on it. Toby proudly told them it was one of the fastest growing youth camps in the country.

Next was Don Kearns, a bush pilot and wilderness guide with a severe jaw and a perpetually downturned mouth that made him look far older than Justin suspected he was. Don had once flown planes for armed forces and now ran a small, wilderness tour company that specialized in the Arctic. He seemed very concerned that a heavy ice storm that was supposed to hit later in the week was now moving in far sooner than expected. His wife, Missy, seemed to be his opposite, with a mass of long, blond curls and a cheery disposition. She was one of the top real estate agents in Saskatoon.

The final pair in their cluster were Scott and Gloria Danis. She was a youthful fiftysomething with vibrant red hair, while Scott was tall, blond and some twenty years her junior. At first Justin assumed they were a May-December romance, until Gloria introduced Scott as her son, who was in the army's Canadian Rangers and filling in this weekend for her husband, who was sick.

They'd been able to glean the names of the other investors who'd be up there this weekend from a group welcome email that the camp had sent out with directions and details on what to pack. Scott was also the only person Justin and Violet had encountered so far that they hadn't expected to be there and hadn't already run a complete background check on.

"My son could use some advice," Gloria told the group. "He just told me on the drive up that he's planning on proposing to his girlfriend this Valentine's Day and hasn't figured out how he's going to do it."

Justin glanced at Scott. The young man was blushing slightly, but his grin was wide and seemed genuine.

"See, my husband and I met at the same camp we own today," Gloria went on. "We were twelve, and it was love at first sight. We'd spend all year writing each other letters and talking on the phone, counting the days until camp came around and we could see each other again. He asked me to marry him when we were just sixteen years old and volunteering as junior counselors. We were sitting in a canoe on the lake at the time, and he gave me this ring he'd made in the craft hut. Got married at camp the summer I went to nursing college, and never looked back."

"Now, how am I ever going to compete with a story like that?" Scott chuckled.

Laughter spread through the group. Justin wasn't sure if it was the height or the smile, but there was just something about Scott that reminded him of "the other guy" every time Justin had discovered the girl he liked had a crush on somebody else.

"Well, I'm afraid I can't help you," Toby spoke first. "We were sitting in my car in the driveway in front of Carol's house one night when I blurted out that I wanted to marry her, and that was that. The next day she called me up and told me I had to go to the mall and get her a ring immediately."

"I'd already told all my friends and family we were getting married." Carol blushed.

More laughter.

"Don took me rock climbing." Missy took his arm and squeezed it tightly. "He flew me to this incredibly remote valley, we scaled the cliffside, and when we got to the top there was this whole picnic spread out with roses and everything. He got down on one knee. It was only later I realized he must've climbed up there already earlier in the day to set it all up."

Despite his dour exterior, Don smiled at his wife affectionately.

"My calves ached for days," he admitted.

The laughter grew. Then as if on cue all eyes in the circle turned to Justin and Violet. Sudden stage fright swept over him. He hadn't planned for this. His mouth opened, but no words came out. So instead, he quickly threw one arm over Violet's shoulders in the hopes it would hide how flustered he felt.

"It doesn't really matter," Justin said. "I was just thankful she said yes."

"Actually, it's really quite the story." Violet slid out from under his arm. "He invited me to this drive-in concert in the park for one of my favorite local bands. It was at the same sledding hill where we'd had our first date."

Justin remembered that date well. The hill had been covered with couples and families sliding down the hill together. He'd expected to steer the toboggan, he remembered, with Violet along as the passenger. To his surprise, she'd suggested they each get their own sled and race them.

"He backed the truck in," Violet went on. "We were sitting on the flatbed in the dark, with this big pepperoni pizza, when suddenly he said he had to go do something. He hopped off the truck and took off. So I was there all alone when suddenly the concert started and there he was up on stage, holding the microphone, asking me to marry him. Next thing I know people are climbing out of vehicles and standing on every truck waving candles. Turned out the whole thing was a setup and the entire audience was made up of our friends, family and colleagues." A smile crossed her lips that came nowhere near touching her eyes. "It was really thoughtful and romantic."

It was also the truth. But as the group of strangers oohed and aahed and congratulated him on the big romantic gesture, something in her eyes made him doubt himself. Had there been something wrong about the way he'd proposed?

The door to the far-left side of the room opened. Frank and Emelia walked into the building, with some kind of bundle that he could only assume was the baby in Emelia's arms. Both were platinum blond, with blue eyes. But that was where the similarities ended. Frank was tall, handsome and imposing. Emelia was pale with a nervous and fragile energy that made Justin instantly worried for her. The door swung open again and Ariel walked in, lugging a huge diaper bag. She was slight, with long dark hair trailing down her back. All three wore the same bright green camp jackets.

It was only then that Emelia turned toward him, and his eyes alighted on the small bundle swathed in a cream snowsuit and white blanket that she was clutching to her chest as if terrified of dropping it. All noise and motion in the room seemed to stop around Justin as his eyes confirmed what his gut had been telling him for days.

Emelia was holding Sadie's son.

His kidnapped nephew whom they'd been searching desperately for ever since he was stolen and sold was there in the same room just a few feet away.

Violet watched as Justin froze, almost as if his internal operating system had suddenly started rebooting. Casually, she turned toward the sandwich plate on the table as her eyes darted up to see what Justin was looking at. Despite all her professional training, something still twisted in her chest as she looked to see the tiny baby in Emelia's arms.

Hi, little guy. I promise to do everything in my power to bring you home and keep you safe.

"Hey, everyone!" Lorenzo strode toward them. "If you want to grab a last bite and take a seat, I think we're going to get started."

"Wait." Violet handed her phone to Justin. "Babe! Can you take a quick picture first? This place is something else."

She pressed the cell phone into Justin's fingers, then signaled Missy, Carol and Gloria to join her. The women gamely posed as Lorenzo theatrically knelt in front of them holding a plate of sandwiches.

Justin held up the camera and smiled, like an actor who'd just remembered his role. He took shots from multiple angles as they all laughed and smiled. Then the group checked out the pictures. They were good. He'd even managed to catch both the fireplace and falling snow. It wasn't until everyone moved to the circle of chairs that Violet had the privacy to zoom in on the family in the back of the picture. He'd gotten a good clear shot of Frank, Emelia and Ariel. But between the snowsuit, the blanket and Frank's protective stance, they could barely see more than Matty's nose.

Staff and guests took their seats. Violet and Justin sat to the left side of the circle, closest to the door the DuBois couple had come through. Frank and Ariel both sat and joined the group. But Emelia stood behind Frank, holding the baby and shifting her weight like she wasn't sure what to do.

"Welcome, everyone!" A man with a booming voice and the look of a triathlete Santa stood at the front of the semicircle. "I'm Ross Halton, owner of the Mount Prince Wilderness Resort. Let me just start off by thanking you all for coming here this weekend, from across the country. I know we're not the easiest place to get to. I also want to thank our dedicated staff, who will be showing you around this weekend, especially as I know for some of you it'll be your last weekend with us before you head off to new adventures."

"No worries." Frank crossed his arms over his broad chest. "I know I'm speaking for everyone when I say there's nowhere else we'd rather be."

But why are you still here if you just bought a stolen baby?

Or do you not know your baby was stolen?

The questions ran unanswered in circles around Violet's brain.

Ross sat down and asked everyone to go around the circle and introduce themselves. But they'd barely gotten a quarter of the way when Matty started to wail. It was a high-pitched and uncomfortable cry. Justin winced, and instinctively Violet reached for his hand. She squeezed his fingers, and he squeezed hers back.

"You should get your little one out of his snowsuit," Carol said loudly. "The poor baby has got to be boiling in that thing."

"Just take him back to the cabin, honey," Frank said. "It's got to be close to his nap time." He looked around the group with a proud smile. "Sorry, everyone. We just became new parents, and neither of us have been getting much sleep in the past few days. He's a tricky baby."

Understanding smiles beamed around the circle. Violet watched as Emelia picked up the large diaper bag and disappeared back through the side door, taking Matty with her. Introductions continued, then Ross outlined the various activities that would be taking place. Violet still hadn't let go of Justin's hand, and he was still holding hers, too, as if for joint moral support as they both battled the urge to leap up and run after Emelia. But she couldn't see a way either of them could do so without raising suspicion and potentially blowing their cover.

Lord, help me to be patient and trust Your timing.

The briefing continued for a while. Then Lorenzo

hooked up a laptop and projector screen, as other staff pulled down blinds over the towering windows and dimmed the lights. Ross explained they were about to watch a video about the history of the camp. Violet watched as Frank whispered something to Ariel. The nurse got up and slipped through the side door. All eyes turned as music swelled and faces of happy adventurers filled the screen. Violet leaned toward Justin.

"Cover me," she whispered. "I'm going to try to talk to Ariel."

He nodded, and Violet slipped across the room and through the side door, fighting the urge to look back and see if anyone was watching her go. The door led to a small storage room lined with shelves packed with sporting goods, staff gear and climbing harnesses. At first, she didn't see Ariel anywhere. Then the other woman reappeared from deep within the shelves. She was struggling with a giant bucket filled with the kind of rock salt used for melting ice.

"Oh, hi!" Ariel startled and dropped the bucket at her feet. But within an instant a pretty smile crossed her face and a flush rose to her cheeks. "Can I help you find something?"

"No, thanks," Violet said. "I just wanted to step outside to get a quick breath of air. My stomach still feels a bit rattled from the long drive here."

"I get that," Ariel said. "I've never been one for sitting still, and Ross can be a bit long-winded."

"Do you need a hand with that?"

Ariel looked down at the rock salt.

"It is kind of a monster of a bucket," Ariel said. "It's

not actual salt, by the way. We used to use real salt, but then I told Lorenzo it was bad for the wildlife, and he switched it for an eco-friendly substitute salt. But it's still just as heavy."

"Please, let me help you with it," Violet said. "Honestly, you'd be doing me a favor. My husband, Josh, is back in there covering everything for us, and I'd much rather help you spread some fake-salt around outside than listen to a presentation on projected budgetary shortfalls. It feels too much like math class."

"Okay, then." Ariel's tone was upbeat, even joyful. "In that case, if you can help me out, that would be awesome."

Ariel grabbed a green jacket off a hook by the door and slid it on. It was only then Violet realized that while she still had her boots on, she'd have to go back into the main room and dig her coat off the hook.

"You want to borrow a staff jacket?" Ariel asked, as if reading her mind. "They're really warm and waterproof. Plus, this stuff can stain your clothes." She dug into her pockets and pulled out a pair of gloves. "I've got a spare pair of gloves, too, which you can borrow."

"Thank you." Violet grabbed a green jacket off the rack, put it on then took the gloves Ariel offered her.

"Just return them to me when you see me later. Or leave them here on the shelf."

The bucket had two handles, one on either side. Ariel dropped two scoops into the bucket, took one of the handles and pushed the door open. Violet took the other handle and followed.

"Where are we going?"

"My best friend, Emelia, just had a baby. His name is Matty. She's the one who just popped by orientation with her husband, Frank. Ross asked everyone on-site to be there to help build up the place." A narrow path lay ahead of them through the trees. Ariel steered them up it. "They live in a cottage up this way, and the path was so slippery that Emelia almost fell when we came down. So Frank asked me to come lay some salt down to make the path safer."

Something in her tone implied Ariel wasn't exactly impressed that big, strong Frank wasn't salting the ground himself. The path was barely more than a foot wide and so treacherously steep that Violet found herself constantly watching her step. The heavy bucket swung back and forth, shifting its weight with each step and forcing Violet to readjust her grip. Ariel stumbled forward and nearly dropped the bucket.

"Are you okay?" Violet asked.

"Yeah, I'm just tired. I've been helping out with the baby a lot."

She couldn't imagine how Ariel would've lugged the bucket alone.

"You're a nurse, right?"

"Nurse practitioner." Ariel tossed fake-salt in front of them as they went. "Which means I can do a lot of the same things a doctor can, like give diagnoses, prescribe medications and do medical procedures."

Also deliver and register the birth of a baby.

The trees parted on their right, and Violet looked down to see a steep slope plunging beside them, with nothing but a simple wooden railing stopping them from sliding over the edge. Ariel followed her gaze.

"Frank always says he's skied steeper slopes than that."

Ariel sounded skeptical. Violet got the impression that for as close as Ariel felt to her friend Emelia, the same didn't extend to Emelia's husband.

"Did I hear that you're leaving?"

"I am," Ariel said. They navigated their way around a sharp corner, passed a fork in the path and then continued up the mountain. "Frank got this amazing new job at a camp in Scandinavia, close to his family, and Emelia asked me to go with them as their nanny. She used to work in the front office, and we got really close. I just love her and baby Matty to bits. Plus, I've never really traveled, and Frank promised me lots of time off to explore Europe."

Some people were just naturally chatty, and Ariel struck her as one of them. Nothing in their conversation would've struck Violet as out of the ordinary, were it not for the heinous crime she suspected Ariel was helping cover up.

An A-framed cottage appeared ahead through the trees, nestled at the top of a mountain peak. Ariel set the bucket down next to a flight of wooden stairs that led up to the front porch. Violet looked around. The ground sloped downward in all directions. It would be nearly impossible for someone to sneak up on the cottage without being seen. Ariel dug her scoop into the bucket and started scattering the fake-salt over the steps.

"Is your cabin around here, too?" Violet asked.

"I used to bunk with a couple of the other single women," Ariel said. "But I moved in with Emelia when she became pregnant. It was a difficult pregnancy. Frank was overseas, and she had trouble keeping food down. She asked me to stay after Matty was born. Emelia still has health problems, and Frank gets really impatient when Matty cries, so having an extra pair of hands helps." Then something flickered in Ariel's eyes as if she'd just caught herself saying more than she should. "Emelia's an amazing mother, though. She loves Matty so much. She wanted a baby for a really long time, and when Matty came along it felt…" Her voice drifted off as she searched for the right word. "Almost too good to be true."

A baby's cry filled the air. They turned toward the cottage. There in the upper window she could see the silhouette of Emelia bouncing baby Matty.

"He sounds hungry." Worry filled Ariel's face.

"You go." Violet waved her toward the cottage. "The bucket's pretty much empty, and I can take it back to the lodge."

"You sure?"

"Absolutely," Violet said. "Go help your friend."

"Thanks so much!" Ariel turned and ran up the steps. "You're really awesome, and I owe you one!"

Ariel disappeared through the door. Violet dumped the scoops inside the bucket, pulled her hood up over her head and started back down toward the lodge. Her eyes rose to the glimpses of blue sky that peeked through the trees.

Help me, Lord. I'm so conflicted right now. To be

honest, I kind of like Ariel. But if we're right, she committed a terrible crime.

Violet's footsteps slipped and slid as she stumbled down the path through the trees, then she carefully picked her way along the long open stretch that ran beside the slope Frank apparently liked to brag he could ski.

However Ariel thought Matty had come into their lives, she definitely saw it as a blessing. How many times had Violet herself wanted something—even begged God for it in prayer—when the answer had been no? But she'd never once considered committing a crime to make her own dreams come true.

Let alone tried to steal somebody else's blessing and make it her own.

It seemed that whatever crimes Ariel may have committed, she fully believed she'd done the right thing. What did that mean?

A loud crack sounded in the forest. Violet spun toward the sound in time to see a dark shape move through the trees. There was a bang like a firecracker going off, then a roaring sound as a mass of ice, snow and rocks cascaded down toward her, like a fast-moving stream cutting through the forest.

She turned to run. But it was too late.

In an instant the mini-avalanche had enveloped her, knocking her off her feet and sweeping her over the edge.

FOUR

It was like a wave buffeting against her body, stealing her balance and leaving her at the mercy of the current. *Help me, Lord!* Violet slid down the hill, desperately trying to dig her feet into the snow to slow her descent while her hands struggled to grab ahold of anything she could. Her back slammed hard into a tree that was growing horizontally out of the slope. In a desperate motion, she twisted her body toward the trunk, wrapped all four limbs around it and held on tight, until the rush of falling snow around her stopped.

Then Violet gritted her teeth, gasped a painful breath and looked up. She'd stopped sliding, but now she was suspended partway down the slope, maybe twenty feet from the railing.

Thank You, God. If she'd tumbled all the way down to the bottom she could've been injured, stranded down there or worse.

Now what?

Instinctively she opened her mouth to call for help then caught herself. This mini-avalanche was no accident. She'd seen a figure in the trees just before the rush of snow had started toward her. What if he was still up there? A cold wind cut through the air. Her body ached from the strain of bracing herself against the tree. She scanned the slope above her. The climb back up would be tricky not to mention dangerous. But not insurmountable. And she couldn't just hang on the side of the mountain forever. A pine tree, wider and sturdier than the one she now clung to, sat a couple of feet above her to her right. Carefully, Violet slid her feet beneath her and crouched. Then slowly and painfully, she shimmied her way across the slope, to the larger tree, inch by inch, using rocks and roots as footholds until she managed to grab ahold of its rough branches. She climbed her way up onto the trunk. Pine needles scraped against her skin. But the ledge was only ten feet beneath her now.

"Viv!" Justin's faint voice drifted toward her on the wintry air.

Relief filled her chest. But still she hesitated. If she called back would she be putting Justin's life in danger? Then she heard more voices calling her name and realized Justin wasn't alone. Surely whoever had caused her to fall wouldn't attack Justin in front of witnesses.

"Viv!" Justin shouted again. "Babe! Where are you?"

"I'm here!"

"I'm coming!"

She heard the sound of footsteps. Then she saw a man lowering himself over the ledge to reach her, his form a dark and featureless silhouette against the bright sun.

"Hey, are you okay? What are you doing down here?" She blinked and her eyes adjusted. It wasn't Justin. It was Lorenzo. "Grab my hand and I'll haul you up."

Lorenzo's fingers hovered a few inches above hers. She'd have to jump for it and trust the camp's chief of operations wouldn't let her fall.

But was he involved in this? Could she trust him?

"Hey, Viv!" Justin's relieved face appeared over the edge, peering down at her. "You okay?"

His eyes flickered from her face to Lorenzo and back again, and it was as if she could see her own fears about trusting Lorenzo reflected back in his eyes.

She took a deep breath and reminded herself she wasn't a cop right now, and Lorenzo wasn't a suspect. She was Viv Cooper of Dukes Wilderness Adventures being offered a helping hand by someone who worked at a camp she was considering investing in.

She glanced at Lorenzo. "Ready?"

"Yup. We got this. Team effort."

"On the count of three." Violet braced herself to jump. "One, two…" *Lord, please keep me safe.* "Three!"

She sprung, leaving the security of the tree trunk and letting Lorenzo grab her right hand, then Justin grabbed her left and together the men pulled her over the ledge, past the broken railing. As soon as her knees hit solid ground again, Lorenzo let go, but Justin didn't. Instead, Justin took both of her hands and helped her to her feet.

"Are you okay?" Worry pooled in his eyes.

"I'm all right." Then without stopping to question why, she instinctively pulled her hands from his, wrapped her arms around his neck and hugged him. Justin hesitated, then hugged her back. She could feel his heartbeat through his chest. It was racing.

"I'll fill you in when we're alone," she whispered to him.

"Why is she wearing a staff jacket?" Frank asked. Violet pulled back, and it was only then she realized Frank was there, too, standing a few feet behind Justin. "Is Ross giving them out now? They're not exactly new."

She'd forgotten she was wearing the same bright green jacket as the rest of the Mount Prince staff. Had someone mistaken her for Ariel from a distance? They were a similar height, and both had long dark hair. Justin followed her gaze.

"Lorenzo and I were standing outside when the video wrapped up—" Justin raised his voice loud enough that the others were included in the conversation "—when Lorenzo got a call from Ariel on the walkie-talkie saying she'd spotted a small avalanche and was worried you'd fallen over the edge. We raced here, and Frank followed us."

So it wasn't possible either Lorenzo or Frank had been the figure she'd seen in the woods.

"I thought I'd mentioned in the security briefing that some of the paths were unstable, and it was best not to go outside the main area on your own," Lorenzo said, almost apologetically. "But Ariel said she'd been struggling with the bucket, and you'd agreed to help. What happened?"

Violet prayed for wisdom. She hadn't gotten a good look at the figure in the trees. Nobody knew she'd even seen them but her. And for now, catching whoever knocked her over the edge was secondary to getting a sample of Matty's DNA.

"My stomach was bugging me, so I slipped out of the back for bit of fresh air to settle my system and offered to help Ariel salt the path. She was kind enough to lend me a staff jacket and keep me company. She said the fake-salt product you use could stain my clothes. I'd been admiring the view when suddenly I got hit by a mini-avalanche and lost my footing. Really, I just feel so silly and embarrassed about the whole thing."

"Well, it was good of you to help her." She glanced at Frank, but he wasn't even looking at her. Despite Frank's reputation as a philanderer, Violet, with her now dirty staff jacket, scratched glasses and hair full of pine needles, might as well have been invisible. "My wife and child are the most important thing in the world to me, and I'd do anything to keep them safe from harm. Now, I'd better check in to see if they're okay and tell them to stay put at the cottage until we get the railing fixed."

Frank started up the path, without saying goodbye.

Lorenzo turned to Violet and Justin.

"I'm sorry about all this," Lorenzo said. "As I'm sure you know, mini-avalanches are rare, but they do happen when there's been a heavy buildup of snow like there's been this season. We should head back to the lodge. Are you good to walk?"

"I'm fine. Thank you."

The three of them walked back down through the woods together single file, with Lorenzo leading the way and Justin taking up the rear. For a while they were quiet, each of them lost in their own thoughts and listening to the sound of their feet crunching in the snow and the wind brushing the trees. Then Justin snorted.

Violet stopped. So did Lorenzo.

Her eyebrows rose. "What's so funny?"

Justin actually managed to look embarrassed.

"I'm sorry. This is really petty of me, and I'm almost ashamed to admit it out loud. But I actually recognized Frank as one of the heirs to the DuBois Oil and Gas fortune. And I found it ironic that a man who's that wealthy and worried about his family is complaining about something as easily fixed as a bad railing. It couldn't have gotten that worn down overnight. Why hasn't he stepped up and offered to help replace it before? Or for that matter helped with any of the other little repairs this place needs that would've impacted his wife and kid?"

Lorenzo gave a wry and somewhat knowing grin, as if the thought had crossed his mind as well and he knew the answer to the question. They turned and continued down the hill.

"I'm not going to tells stories that aren't mine to share." Lorenzo's voice dropped. "But Frank's made several trips overseas to visit his grandmother in the past year, apparently to ask for money, and Ariel has told me some stuff about their situation. Let's just say, coming from a wealthy family doesn't necessarily mean you get a share of the dough. I don't know if it's true, but Ariel even said once that she thinks he might have been cut out altogether if it wasn't for him becoming a father."

Frank wouldn't have inherited his family's money if he hadn't produced a child? Why?

Once again, questions filled Justin's mind. Lorenzo

parted ways with them as they reached the bottom of the hill, and the triangle was sounding again, summoning them all to the lodge.

Justin glanced around. Potential investors and staff were making their way back, but none who were close enough yet to eavesdrop on their conversation.

"Sadly, I'm guessing there's no way we can just slip off to our cabin to talk?" Justin whispered to Violet.

"Not without risking our cover or drawing any more unwanted attention to ourselves. As it is, I don't know how I'm going to explain why I look like I got dragged through a bush backward."

"You look fine." More than fine, she looked beautiful. Her face was flushed from the outdoors, and the tinted lenses she was wearing did little to hide her dazzling eyes. He reached up and pulled a small pine cone from her hair. "I discovered an emergency exit by the kitchen. I'll slip in the front door, grab your coat and then meet you by the back door so you can freshen up without anyone noticing. There are washrooms down that way, too."

"But won't people notice you grabbing my coat and taking it down the hallway?"

"Nah. I've got this."

For a moment he thought she was going to argue with him. Instead, she turned and dashed around the side of the building. He strode through the front door, with his head held high and purpose in his step, being careful not to meet anyone's eye.

When he opened the back door he found Violet waiting for him between the row of trash cans and woodpile.

He propped the door open while she quickly changed her coat, then she pulled a small comb and compact from her pocket and fixed her hair.

"Did anybody see you?" she asked.

"Oh, probably. But, you know as well as I do, the trick to undercover work is not to be invisible but forgettable. There were a smattering of other people in the lodge, but they were all busy in their own conversations or doing their own thing, so I was able to take advantage of their blind spots in perception."

She turned and stared at him.

"I didn't know you had any undercover training."

"Actually," Justin said. "I scored so high in interpersonal skills during basic training that Zablocie tried to recruit me to do undercover work for major crimes. Special Victims Unit specifically."

"How come you never told me that?"

Because you and your brother both excelled in that kind of hands-on police work, but I couldn't hack it, and I didn't want you thinking less of me.

Ross's voice boomed down the hall, telling whoever was in hollering range that they were about to get started.

"I'll tell you later. We've got to go."

They left the borrowed jacket and gloves in a supply closet and joined the others in the main room. It was a smaller contingency of staff this time, Justin noted, that didn't include Frank, Emelia, Ariel or Lorenzo. Ross led them on a walking tour of the wider property, pointing out some of the main buildings inside the complex and giving everyone the opportunity to try out the indoor climbing wall and play a few rounds on the curling rink. Then they strapped themselves into snowshoes for a hike around the broader paths. Justin mapped them out in his mind as they went, noting which ones led where and the simple system of colored paint splotches on trees they used to mark the paths. Ross pointed out an outdoor zip line and climbing course that were shut down for the season, a small frozen pond that served as a swimming hole in the summer and an ice hockey rink for shimmy games in the winter.

"What about the ski lifts?" Don pointed through the wires that strung toward trees to their right.

The group was standing at a fork in the trees between the green circular path that led back to the lodge and the white one leading to the tobogganing hill.

"Oh, they're on our list of areas of improvement." Ross chuckled, which Justin took as a euphemism for the fact they were out of commission.

"Can we see the sledding hill?" Toby asked. "I heard it's one of the smoothest and longest in Canada."

"Sadly, without the gondolas working, once you get down to the bottom it's a long hike back up. But Lorenzo keeps a snowmobile in the first aid shed at the bottom, so we're covered if any campers try to make an unexpected trip down." Ross turned and pointed in the opposite direction to their left. "Not to spoil the surprise, but we'll be back here tomorrow after breakfast for some winter rock climbing. We have some wonderful cliffs and a full array of winter climbing gear just this way."

"As long as the storm holds," Don interjected. "As a

pilot I'm quite accustomed to watching the skies, and I think we're going to get quite the dumping tonight. Possibly some freezing rain as well."

Ross nodded vaguely. "Well, we do get all kinds of weather up here. Now come on, we're heading this way." He steered them past the broken ski lift, unusable sledding hill and the cliffs they might see tomorrow.

The day wore on, and Justin watched the tapestry of thick white clouds blanket the skies above them, like someone had unspooled a roll of quilter's cotton across the sky. With each passing hour, Justin found himself growing more and more uneasy. He hadn't seen his nephew since the welcome reception. And as long as some combination of Frank, Emelia or Ariel were holed up in their cabin, it would be near impossible to sneak in and get something with Matty's DNA on it without being caught.

He was hoping they'd make an appearance for dinner, so that either he or Violet could head to the cabin then, while it was empty. But unfortunately, Ross had planned a formal sit-down dinner for the investors, with none of the other staff present except for a gray-haired man in wire-framed glasses whom Ross introduced as his chief financial officer.

Justin could practically feel Violet's frustration radiating through her at how the afternoon had unfolded as they took their seats at the long table in the lodge. Her smile was tight, almost forced, and as he reached for her hand under the table to give her a quick and reassuring squeeze her fingers were as stiff as if they'd been frozen. To be fair, his own desire to leap up, run to the cottage, snatch up his nephew and rescue him from harm burned like fire through Justin's veins.

God, please help us get what we need and fast. You know I've never been good at sitting still when somebody I care about is in trouble.

Platters laden with meat, potatoes, vegetables and bread were passed around. Ross sat at the head of the table and clinked his glass like a family patriarch welcoming them to holiday dinner.

"I know you guys got a lot of information today, so I thought it would be good to have a little question-and-answer session over dinner in case there was anything more you wanted to know about."

Justin stabbed a thick roll with his butter knife. The only question he had in his mind was why Ross had kept Lorenzo out of the whole tour and dinner, when Lorenzo seemed to be the one who had a much stronger sense of what day-to-day operations were like around the place. Unless the answer was as simple as Ross wanted to manage the camp's image.

"I have a concern actually." Missy, the blond real estate agent, and wife of bush pilot Don, leaned forward. When they'd met earlier, Justin had assumed she was the sunny one of the couple. But now she was all business. "We've only been touring a very small selection of the buildings on this property, and while it's nice to talk about making exterior renovations—like fresh coats of paint and a shiny new ice hockey rink—if there are fundamental problems with this place's structures and foundations, it's all going to crumble no matter how much money you throw at it."

She went on to ask specific questions about surveys and assessments, and while they didn't make a lot of sense to Justin, he couldn't help but notice the financial officer paled slightly.

"I'm really glad you brought that up," Violet said. "Because while I don't have a background like yours, I've been noticing the rodent traps and ratty furniture and wondering if it was just petty little stuff or if it was a sign that something deeper was wrong."

Now, wasn't that the truth.

"We'll follow up with you after the weekend and get you everything you need," Ross replied, lightly. "Anyone else?"

"You talked a lot about wanting to attract churches and youth groups," Toby said. "But I didn't hear much of a plan beyond building a couple of new bunk rooms and reminding your staff about watching their language."

"Surface stuff," his wife, Carol, added.

People nodded and murmured in agreement.

It seemed like a theme was developing here.

"What was missing from your presentation so far," Toby went on, "was any kind of deeper understanding of why a community would want to come together at a place like this."

"Actually, Lorenzo and I had a pretty good chat about that," Scott chimed in. "We talked about my time in the Canadian Rangers and his time at youth camps, growing up. I think he really gets the importance of teamwork in building community."

"See, I'd like to hear more about that." Toby pointed his finger approvingly at Scott.

"I know I'm the outsider," Scott added, looking around the table, "as I'm the only one here who's not in full-time camp work. But I find it's hard to build trust without honesty and vulnerability. Right now it feels like you're hiding your flaws. We can't work with you if we don't even know who you are."

Justin leaned back and listened as one potential investor after another grilled Ross about what exactly they'd seen as wrong in the place. One of the questions he'd had going into the investigation was how Emelia had been able to fake her pregnancy and get a baby smuggled in without getting caught. Now a picture was forming in his mind of a camp with some well-meaning but overwhelmed staff and an owner who was clueless about what was happening on the ground.

"How about you, Josh?" Scott asked, pointedly as the meal was wrapping up. "I can't help but notice you've been pretty quiet."

Justin forced a chuckle that he hoped sounded casual and light. "Honestly? Everyone's done such a great job of flagging things they're concerned about, and I've just been taking it all in."

"Okay," Scott said, and Justin wasn't quite sure what to make of it.

As dinner ended, they were all escorted outside where a large bonfire had been built in the wide-open space in front of the lodge. Lorenzo reappeared with a guitar. He flashed them both a big smile and a thumbs-up, as if to signal to Justin and Violet that the railing had been fixed.

As they all sat on wooden logs around the fire, Violet

leaned against Justin. Her head brushed his shoulder, and the warmth of her filled his core.

"I know you're frustrated," she whispered softly into his ear. "I am, too. But it's going to be okay. We're in this together, and I have faith in us."

And until that moment he'd never realized how much something inside him had longed to hear those words, back when they'd been engaged. How much he'd hoped that if he opened up to her about everything he was going through, she'd look at him and say that it was going to be okay, and she had faith in them.

The bright orange flames danced in her gaze, as the fire licked up toward the sky. The music of the circle around them seemed to fade away as if for a moment nothing else existed but her. He found himself leaning toward her. But before Justin knew what he'd have even done if he'd let his lips get close enough to kiss Violet's mouth, the freezing rain began to fall. Thick and relentless drops stung their skin, soaked their heads and sent up smoke as they sizzled in the fire.

The music stopped as people leaped to their feet and ran for the safety of the lodge. A s'mores station was quickly set up by the fireplace, which Justin suspected had been intended for the bonfire outside.

Violet glanced at her phone.

"It's almost nine," she said loudly. "I think we're going to call it a night and get back to our cabin. I promised my brother I'd try and call him before bed."

As if on cue, everyone else pulled their phones from their pockets, checked the screens and made similar comments about calling it a night. The evening disbanded shortly afterward.

Violet and Justin sprinted back to their cabin, did a quick perimeter check and watched the hidden video footage. No unwanted visitors or suspicious activity.

Then Violet dialed Anthony and put it on speaker-phone so Justin could listen in. Her first call didn't go through. The signal was weak. Violet's lips moved in silent prayer as she dialed again. But the second call didn't go through, either, and neither did the third. He was about to give up hope when the fourth try began to ring. Then he heard a click and recorded voice say, "The number you have reached is not in service. Please check the number and try your call again. This is a recording."

Violet breathed a sigh of relief, signaled Justin to join her where she stood and punched in a password.

A moment later she heard her brother say, "Hello?"

"Anthony, hi! I'm here with Justin. You're on speak-erphone."

"Hey, sis. Hello, Justin," Anthony said. "I've got Tessa here with me, too."

Tessa called out hello in the background.

Anthony and Tessa had been childhood sweethearts who had reconnected a few months back when Tessa had been accused of murder and Anthony was the RCMP sergeant tasked with tracking her down. Justin had al-ready called off the wedding by then. And when An-thony and Tessa had decided to elope, Violet and Justin had given them their entire wedding and reception book-ing for their special day—venue, catering, music, the lot. Justin would've let them have it for free, if they'd taken it. He was certain Violet would've, too. But Anthony and Tessa hadn't only covered their wedding bills, but had taken some of the heat off Justin and Violet by providing a new topic of gossip for their friends, family and colleagues with their hasty wedding.

"How's it going?" Anthony asked.

"Weak phone signal. Crumbling camp. We got eyes on the child and a visual confirmation that he's Justin's nephew, but no DNA sample yet."

Violet quickly filled them in on seeing Curly spying on their cabin when they'd first arrived and the fact they hadn't seen him since. Then she told them about her conversation with Ariel and her tumble down the hill, although Justin noted she downplayed the danger she'd been in.

"Lorenzo made an odd comment about hearing a rumor Frank was going to be cut out of the family fortune before he had a child," Violet added. "Can you look into that?"

"Absolutely."

"Also, there's an extra investor we didn't vet," Justin said. "Scott Danis is filling in for his dad, who's apparently sick. He's the son of Gloria, in his early twenties and an army ranger."

And I don't think he likes me.

"One second," Anthony said. "A message just came through from Zablocie that he needs me to pass on."

Static crackled down the phone. Minutes ticked past until Justin was worried the call had dropped without them realizing it. Then Anthony was back.

"I have something I need to tell you," Anthony said,

and Justin could tell by his tone it wasn't good news. "The Missing Persons Unit has located the family who purchased baby number two from the L.B. Syndicate. A cleaner had recognized the child from an Amber Alert, smuggled the child out and took her to the closest police station."

"Well, that's really good news," Violet said.

"Yeah." They heard Anthony take in a deep breath and let it out slowly. "Unfortunately, by the time the unit moved in on the home of the family who'd bought the child, they found everybody there dead."

FIVE

"Dead?" Violet repeated. She felt the color drain from her face. Her legs began to buckle. In a swift and smooth motion, Justin stepped toward her. With one hand he took the phone from her fingers, and with the other, he helped her sit down on the couch. "How, Anthony?"

"Carbon monoxide poisoning. Made to look like an accident. Mother, father and two bodyguards dead. No kids involved, thankfully."

Violet let out a long breath.

"It all fits within the theory that the L.B. Syndicate has somebody watching each of the buyer families," Justin said, "at least for a while, to make sure nobody does or says anything that could lead to L.B. getting caught. Somebody recognized the baby and risked their lives to bring it to police. The syndicate moved in and took out the rest of the family before anything could lead back to them. Let me guess, their computers were completely wiped?"

"Yup. But they're being shipped to the cybercrimes unit for analysis. Hopefully you'll be able to get something from them."

"I'll get on it as soon as I'm back," Justin said.

"And again, the baby's okay?" Violet confirmed.

"One hundred percent."

She closed her eyes. *Thank You, God.*

She felt Justin reach for her hand and squeeze it reassuringly. She squeezed him back.

"Now you've seen someone you think is an L.B. Syndicate operative at the camp," Anthony said. "We have to face the possibility that if he thinks Matty's identity has been compromised, he will kill the DuBois family and anyone else they see as a threat."

Like Ariel. Maybe even Lorenzo or other staff and investors. They might even kill Matty. She tightened her grip on Justin's fingers.

"Thankfully we haven't seen Curly for hours," Justin said. "But we can't discount the possibility he's still here at the camp, hiding in one of the empty buildings or being hidden by someone."

"I'm worried this undercover mission has become too dangerous," Anthony said. "I think you should consider calling it off and coming back to headquarters to find a different way to tackle this investigation."

"What?" Violet dropped Justin's hand and stood. "Hang on. You did not just suggest I turn tail and run." Her brother's overprotectiveness was unbelievable. "I'm an RCMP corporal, Anthony, not a tissue-paper princess doll. This is my job, and I'm going to do it." The freezing rain grew heavier outside, beating against the roof of the cabin. The phone line crackled. "Can you honestly tell me that you'd say this to anybody else with my résumé, rank and expertise, who wasn't your sister?"

"Would you be this dismissive of the concerns of any other sergeant in the Major Crimes Unit who wasn't your brother?" he shot back.

"I would if I felt they weren't respecting me!" she retorted.

Anthony paused. Then he let out a low chuckle that sounded more than a little chagrined.

"Fair enough. You're right about that. Maybe I'm being overprotective, and if so, I'm sorry. I knew you wouldn't go for it, but I had to give it a shot. And as you're clearly staying up there, I do think you need closer backup. I get why Zablocie made the call to keep the circle of knowledge on this as small as possible. But I don't like knowing that if something goes wrong it could take me three hours or more to get to you."

Under the circumstances, neither did she.

"There's an RCMP safe house about half an hour's drive from the Mount Prince parking lot," Anthony went on. "With your permission, because this is your operation after all, I'm going to ask Zablocie to sign off on Tessa and me heading up there first thing tomorrow and setting up camp. That way, if things suddenly go south, I'm close."

Violet glanced at Justin. He nodded. Then her eyes drifted past him to the rucksack of baby gear he'd brought up just in case they needed to grab Matty for an emergency extraction. If someone did make an attempt on the baby's life and they had to rescue him and run, it would be nice to have a safe house ready nearby, once they figured out how to get him down the mountain.

"It's a good idea. Yeah, please take that to Zablocie tomorrow."

"Will do," Anthony said.

They wrapped up the call shortly afterward. Justin shifted his weight on the couch, and it let out a plaintive squeak.

"This couch really is terrible. I think I sat directly on a spring. How are you?"

"I'm okay." Violet began to pace the cabin. "More determined and resolved if anything. What about you?"

"Bit shaken. Worried for everyone involved if we botch this." He leaned back and ran both hands over his face and up through his hair as if trying to wipe something from his brain. "Remember I told you that Zablocie had once tried to recruit me for undercover work in Major Crimes?"

"Yeah." She stopped behind the couch. "I was really surprised, honestly, because you'd never mentioned it to me before."

"Well, that's because I couldn't hack it," Justin said. "In my first few months of training for undercover work in Major Crimes, I had to work a mass casualty crime scene, with kids involved. It was really hard. I felt sick for days afterward."

"I'm sorry." Instinctively, her hand reached for his shoulder. But just as her fingers were about to brush the soft fabric of his sweater she stopped herself, pulled back and crossed her arms. No, she couldn't keep reaching out to him. And vice versa. They were drawing close, too close. He'd broken her heart once, and she couldn't let that happen again.

"I went for counseling afterward," Justin said. "They said I'd probably get used to it. But I didn't think I could without losing part of who I am." He turned, and his blue eyes met hers. Sincerity filled their gaze. It was like the room began to shrink around them. "I feel sometimes like there's big sponge inside me that soaks up everybody else's feelings and problems."

"Even mine?" The question escaped her lips before she could catch herself and stop it.

"Especially yours."

Something tightened in her chest. She stepped back and started pacing.

"I can see now what you mean about Anthony being an overprotective brother. I didn't really get it until right now. My own brother, half sister and mother always rely on me to solve their problems, so it didn't click what it could be like to be on the receiving end of somebody else's unwanted attempts to take care of you."

"It's okay." A tight smile crossed her lips. "He loves me, and he means well."

"Sadie told me once I have a habit of saying things are okay when they're not." Justin gestured to Violet's face. "That smile, that one you're making now, is the same smile you had when you were telling everyone about our wedding proposal. I have to know, what did I get wrong that day? I took you to one of your favorite spots, hired your favorite local band, ordered your favorite pepperoni pizza—"

"I don't like pepperoni pizza."

His eyes widened. "You don't?"

What difference did any of this make now? How would talking about ancient history help their case?

"No. I don't. But the first time you bought it for us, you seemed so excited about it that I just went along with it. My favorite is ham and pineapple—" His mouth opened, but she kept going before he could get a word in edgewise. "Which I knew you didn't like. So instead of just telling you that and ordering two different pizzas, I didn't say anything. Because I dislike conflict even more than pepperoni."

She started pacing again.

"Also, while I'm being really honest, I didn't want a big marriage proposal. I also didn't want a big wedding. I don't like being the center of attention."

Justin stood slowly. Something cooled behind his eyes. Had she hurt him by not being more honest about this kind of stuff before? Maybe.

"But none of that really matters now," Violet said, firmly, not really sure if she was talking to him or to herself. "All that matters right now is this case. Ariel seems to think Matty's arrival was some kind of amazing and unbelievable blessing. If she's in on the crime, which she has to be since she's the one who faked the birth registration, she definitely believes she did the right thing. Also mentioned that Emelia is frequently sick. My take on Ariel is that she's a very positive person who really cares about Emelia and Matty but isn't that impressed with Frank. She specifically said Frank gets impatient when Matty cries."

"Not exactly the sign of a good parent."

Thankfully, he seemed to be okay with how quickly

she'd pulled a one-eighty and steered the conversation away from their past.

"He hardly seems to care about his wife or child, does he?" Violet asked. "So I'll be interested to see what Anthony and Tessa manage to dig up about his family inheritance."

"Me, too," Justin said. "Anything else on Ariel?"

"No, that's all I got on her for now," Violet said. "What's your take on the others?"

"Lorenzo seems like a decent guy." Justin shrugged. "But I can't be sure. Ross looks like he's clueless about what's going on at his camp, in a negligent way. Nothing appears off with any of the investors—"

"Except," Violet interjected, "am I right in thinking you don't like Scott, the twentysomething who's planning on proposing to his girlfriend? You seemed to have an odd moment back at the dinner."

"I don't know… Something about him just rubs me the wrong way."

She decided to let that pass.

"I feel like I have more information than I did this morning, but less clarity," Violet said. "Ariel seems too kindhearted to be an accessory to kidnapping. Emelia seems too weak to orchestrate it. And Frank seems too controlling to miss somebody smuggling a baby right under his nose, but too cunning to risk getting caught by going through this whole charade and hanging out in Canada for a few weeks after Matty's 'birth.' He could've just done the handoff in a back alley behind the hospital and fled the county before the Amber Alert was even issued."

She ran both hands through her dark hair and let it fall. Her eyes itched with fatigue. She needed sleep.

"We should sleep in shifts," she said. "One of us can take the bedroom for a bit and try to get some decent shut-eye. The other can stay out here and be our first line of defense if there's any trouble."

"Or I just take the couch," Justin said. "You can keep the bedroom."

"No." She crossed her arms, almost daring him to challenge her on this. "That couch is atrocious, and we both need to be rested for tomorrow."

Her ego was still smarting a little from the way her well-meaning brother had patronized her, and something inside her almost wanted to fight with her former fiancé on whether she was tough enough to sleep on a couch. For a long moment, Justin stared at her without saying anything.

"Okay," he said, finally. "We can take turns." He glanced at his watch. "Breakfast starts in a little over ten hours, and I don't think it'll be a problem with anyone if we're a little late. I suggest we break it into five-hours shifts. Do you want to go first or second?"

"First, if that's okay. I suspect it's going to take me a while to fall asleep, so I might as well toss and turn on the couch."

"Sounds good." Justin wasn't smiling, but he didn't look upset exactly, just tired. She suspected he was every bit as disappointed as she was that their undercover mission would drag on into a second day.

She wanted to hug him, promise him they'd get Matty's DNA tomorrow and maybe also apologize for bringing up the thing about the pizza. Instead, she gave him what she hoped was a reassuring smile. "Good night. Try to get some sleep."

"You, too," he said. "Just promise me if you see or hear anything suspicious, you'll come wake me up and you won't go investigate without me."

"I promise."

Justin disappeared into the other room. Violet did a perimeter sweep and found nothing, then unrolled a sleeping bag and did her best to find a comfortable position on the couch. The warm glow of the coals in the wood-burning fireplace cast a gentle light around the room, which faded to darkness in the corners. Violet closed her eyes and began to pray.

She thanked God that one of the babies had been found and asked for mercy for all those impacted by the death of the family who'd bought her and protection for whomever the L.B. Syndicate targeted next. She prayed for everyone involved in Matty's kidnapping— including Emelia, Frank and Ariel—that justice would be done swiftly and Matty would be rescued safely. She asked God to take care of Sadie, wherever she was holed up, and that God would heal her and get her the help she needed. She asked God to bless all the investors and staff at Mount Prince.

Finally, she prayed for Justin.

Lord, guide him and strengthen him. Help me be the partner he needs on this case.

Maybe it was a good thing she'd brought up the pizza. Because it was just one small, frivolous example of the fact she'd avoided conflict when they'd been together.

She was certain Justin blamed himself for their breakup. She had, too.

But when she'd seen just how stressed out and overwhelmed he was, why hadn't she just sat him down at her kitchen table, told him she was worried about him and asked him to please just be straight about everything that was bothering him? She could've offered to postpone the wedding. Instead, she'd told herself that once they made it across the finish line and got their wedding over with, they'd have plenty of time to talk on their honeymoon.

Violet dozed on and off, fitfully, getting up at least once an hour to scan the empty darkness outside the cabin windows. Eventually she switched from the couch to the floor after the springs had caught her in the back one too many times, and she made a mental note to tell Justin to bring one of the bunk bed mattresses with him when it was his turn to keep watch.

It was shortly before two in the morning when a chilling, wailing sound caught her ears. She crossed the floor, opened the door and listened. The freezing rain had died down, leaving a bitter wind in its place. For a moment nothing but its howl filled her ears, and she wondered if she'd imagined hearing a voice.

But then her heart froze as another unmistakable sound reached her ears.

Somewhere in the darkness someone was crying and calling for help.

Justin sat bolt upright on the narrow bunk bed as he heard the door creak open.

"Justin?" Violet's voice whispered in the darkness.

"I'm here." He swung his legs over the edge, bumping his head on the bunk above him as he sat up. He'd slept fully clothed in his sweater and jeans in case anything happened. "Everything okay?"

"I heard crying. I think someone's in trouble."

He leaped up, rushed into the main living room and threw the front door open. Impenetrable black air surrounded him, and he waited a moment for his eyes to adjust. "I don't hear anything."

"It comes and goes. It sounds like someone crying and calling for help."

Seconds ticked past. Justin strained his ears, and then he heard an unnerving sound that seemed to cut right through his core. When Violet had mentioned crying, he'd subconsciously expected a soft sound. But this sound that rose on the air was wild and terrified, like someone so scared they were incoherent with despair.

Lord, please, help me rescue them! Help me reach them in time!

Violet grabbed his arm, and he suddenly realized the touch of her hand was the only thing that had stopped him from sprinting toward the sound so immediately that he'd forget to put his coat and boots on. He turned back toward the cabin. Violet was already dressed in her winter gear and was holding out his jacket for him.

"Thank you." He slid his arms through the sleeves and stepped into his boots, feeling torn between the urge to tell her to stay in the cabin where she'd be safe and gratitude that she'd kept her promise not to go off investigating alone.

They set off toward the sound, with nothing but the

glow of their flashlights to illuminate their way in the darkness. Wind beat against their bodies. The uneven ground was slick with ice beneath their feet. His mind knew they were passing other cabins and buildings, but they seemed as nothing more than even darker shadows in the night. The voice came and went. Justin swallowed hard and tried to beat down the panic that rose in his chest. The cries were coming from the direction of the lodge and the path that led to the DuBois cottage.

Suddenly, the ground sloped so steeply beneath them that Justin missed his step and barely caught his footing. But Violet was not so fortunate. She pitched forward, grabbed on to his arm for stability then fell, dragging him down with them. They tumbled to the ground, dropping their flashlights as they went. Justin landed on Violet's legs and heard her wince in pain.

"Get off her!" a male voice shouted in the darkness.

Justin felt a pair of large, gloved hands yank him off Violet and throw him back down into the snow. He leaped up and spun, just as in time to see a tall, muscular silhouette lunge at him. Justin dodged to the side and swung, clocking his attacker hard in the solar plexus. The man grunted as he fell back.

"Stop it!" Violet shouted. "Both of you!"

He was vaguely aware of Violet's voice calling at him to stop. But before he could even respond, the tall man barreled into him, slamming Justin back on the ground. Justin kicked up hard.

"Knock it off!" Violet's voice rose. A bright, blinding flashlight beam shone in his face. "Now! Or I'll leap in there and separate you! We don't have time for this!"

Instinctively, Justin raised his hands to block the light. He blinked, and for the first time, he got a good look at his attacker. It was Scott, the army reservist, whose mother had solicited proposal advice for him.

"Are you all right?" Scott turned to Violet. "We heard screaming, and I ran out here as fast as I could. Did he hurt you?"

The sound of crying had faded again. Justin gritted his teeth and tried to cool his racing blood. The younger man had obviously heard the same cries they had, then seen Justin and Violet on the ground and jumped to conclusions.

"I'm fine! I'd just slipped on the ice and my husband was trying to help me. Josh and I heard the same sound you did and came out to investigate."

Immediately, a flush rose to Scott's face that was so red she could even see it in the glow of the flashlight.

"I am so sorry, man." He turned to Justin and stuck out his hand. "That was totally my fault. I just saw you guys struggling on the ground and got the wrong idea. I hope you can forgive me." Scott rubbed the back of his neck. "It's just that those screams were pretty intense."

"It was." And Justin still wasn't certain where they were coming from.

"Hey!" Another voice shouted from somewhere to their left. They turned to see Don trudging through the snow, with Lorenzo by his side. "Is everything all right? I heard a commotion and then ran into Lorenzo."

Lorenzo's face was as pale as the snow. "I heard crying."

"So did we all," Violet said. "It seems to be coming from somewhere near the lodge."

The five of them set off through the snow, with Lorenzo leading the way. Justin thought he could hear the sound of wailing again, but it was so faint he wasn't sure if it was his own imagination or the person was running out of tears.

They reached the wide-open space in front of the lodge.

Then Justin saw her.

It was Emelia. She was standing by the remains of the bonfire, clad in what looked like long flannel pajamas and a housecoat. She was sobbing.

Justin broke away from the pack and ran toward her, yanking off his coat. He draped it around Emelia's shoulders. But she was shivering so hard her whole body was shaking.

"It's okay," Justin said. "You're safe now."

Was it? Was she?

Emelia turned toward him. Her pale eyes were wide and glazed over, as if she wasn't even sure who he was or what she was looking at.

"You gotta help me," she wailed. "Somebody broke into my cottage! My baby's gone! They've taken Matty!"

SIX

The fear that stabbed Justin's heart was so acute that for a moment he felt unable to breathe. Someone had kidnapped his nephew? Who? How?

"You have to find him!" Emelia's voice rose, as the others reached them. Her eyes were vacant, probably with shock. "They took my baby!"

"We need to call the police," Justin turned to Lorenzo. "Immediately."

"We… I…" Lorenzo hesitated as if struggling over his words. "First, we need to make sure her son is really missing. This isn't the only time she's done something like this. Matty may be safe and sound in his bed."

"You're telling me this isn't the first time she's gone running off in the snow claiming her baby was stolen when it wasn't?" Scott sounded incredulous.

"Well, not exactly." Lorenzo ran his hand over the back of his head. "But she isn't well."

Ariel had told Violet that Emelia was frequently sick, but that was hardly the same thing as believing her child was missing when he wasn't.

Violet joined Justin and helped him hold out his jacket for Emelia to put her arms through.

"Here, Emelia," Violet said, softly. "You'll feel much better with this on, and then we'll figure out what's going on, okay? When did you discover Matty was missing?"

Violet gently coaxed the woman's hand through one sleeve and then the other. Emelia whimpered softly.

"I woke up, and he was gone from his crib."

"What about Frank?" Violet asked. "And Ariel?"

"I checked Frank's room!" Emelia's voice rose. "He's missing, too!" *His room?* Emelia and Frank didn't sleep in the same room? "I pounded on Ariel's door, and she didn't answer! And when I tried her door, it was locked!"

Lorenzo reached to comfort Emelia. Justin let Lorenzo take her.

Justin and Violet stepped back from the group. He wrapped his arm around Violet's shoulder and whispered into her hair. "What do you think is going on?"

"I have no idea," she whispered back. "But we need to get to that cabin, and if Matty is missing, we need to issue an Amber Alert immediately."

"When do we blow our cover?"

"When we have no other choice, and at the last possible second."

"Hello!" Frank ran down the path shouting. "Emelia! Honey! Are you out there?" He ambled into the clearing, clad in full winter gear and holding a large flashlight. He paused and blinked at the small gathering. "Well, hello. What are you all doing here? Have I missed some kind of late-night party?"

Emelia launched herself at Frank. He wrapped one arm around her. Emelia pressed her face into his chest.

"Your wife has been running around in the snow crying for a good fifteen minutes!" Don pushed his way to the front of the group and stood toe-to-toe with Frank. "She says your child is missing!"

"Well, that's ridiculous," Frank said. "Matty's fine. Ariel was just changing his diaper when I left. My wife has terrible nightmares and sleepwalks sometimes."

"She also says you weren't in your room." Scott emphasized *your* like an indictment.

"I sleep in our room, and Emelia likes to stay in Matty's room because he's fussy in the night. Not that it's anybody's business." Frank turned to Lorenzo, and irritation flashed in his eyes. "Why didn't you tell them my wife isn't well and come get me? You know how fragile she is." Then he glanced to his wife. "Emelia, losing control and making a spectacle of yourself this way isn't helping anyone!"

Lorenzo's expression grew so dark he looked capable of punching Frank.

"She needs help," Lorenzo said.

"And she's going to get it, when we move and are closer to family who can help with Matty." Then Frank smiled and raised both hands palms up with an exaggerated shrug. "Show's over, everyone. I appreciate you all getting out of your warm beds to help my wife. But I assure you everything is fine. Now please, go back to your cabins."

But if he'd intended to lighten the mood, it didn't work.

"Their cabin is only a short walk through the trees

and up the mountain." Violet started for the path. "Why don't we all go together and see for ourselves that everything's okay?"

Frank didn't even look her way or acknowledge her words. But thankfully, both Don and Scott were quick to insist that they weren't going back to their cabins until they'd seen for themselves that Matty was all right. Then Lorenzo pointed out that Emelia was wearing Justin's coat, and it was hardly right to send him back to the cabin without it. So the seven of them trudged through the trees to the DuBois cabin together, single file. When they passed the spot where Violet had been knocked down the slope, Justin couldn't help but notice the single-railing fence had been replaced with a much thicker triple-railed one.

"Are you okay?" Violet whispered to Justin. "You must be freezing."

"Honestly, I'm too numb to feel anything right now. I'm just afraid of what we're going to find when we get there."

The lights of the DuBois cottage flickered between the trees. The front door came into view.

"Ariel!" Frank cupped his hands around his mouth and shouted. "Ariel, can you get out here please and bring the baby. Apparently our guests want the reassurance that he's alive and well."

"It's better if we come in," Justin called. "Don't bring the baby out in this cold."

But Frank didn't even seem to have heard him. The cottage's outdoor light switched on. Bright light flooded the porch. The door swung open. Ariel stood in the doorway, cradling Justin's nephew in her arms. The baby waved his arms and fussed. Violet gasped. Justin could hear the other men who'd come up with them murmuring something unintelligible under their breaths. Emelia let out a cry and ran across the snow, nearly falling as her feet slipped on the icy ground. She ran up the cottage's front steps, took Matty from Ariel and gathered him into her arms.

"Matty!" Tears streamed down her face. "You're all right! I thought they had taken you."

Frank turned toward the others.

"See, folks, I told you everything was fine," he said with a tight-lipped smile. "Now, please head back to your cabins and let my family have some privacy."

Violet pulled Justin back from the others.

"What's going on?" Violet whispered.

Justin shook his head. "I have no idea."

About twenty minutes later Violet and Justin were back in their cabin, sitting side by side on the floor in front of the wood-burning stove. She unzipped her coat and peeled off her scarf, hat and gloves. But Justin was still so bundled up he hadn't even taken his boots off.

"How are you feeling?" Violet asked.

If she had to guess, he'd been outside without his coat on for roughly fifteen minutes, and while that hadn't been enough to threaten his life, it still had to be a serious jolt to his system.

"Numb."

"Physically or emotionally?"

"Both." Justin leaned back against the couch and slowly unfurled his limbs. "What just happened?"

It was the third or fourth time he'd asked her some variation of that question ever since they'd seen baby Matty safe and well in Ariel's arms. Violet still didn't have an answer for him.

"I wish I knew," Violet said.

"Do you believe Frank was telling us the truth?" Justin asked. "About Emelia having nightmares and sleepwalking?"

"No."

"Neither do I. But that still doesn't get me any closer to figuring out what the truth actually is."

"Ariel did tell me that Emelia had been sick a lot. Couldn't keep food down when she was pregnant. Only we know she wasn't actually pregnant. She looks weak and shaky. But I don't know how hallucinations could fit into that."

"Do you think it's possible that Curly or somebody else snatched Matty and then put him back when Emelia ran for help?"

"I don't know. Maybe."

Neither of them had seen Curly since Violet had spotted him outside their window hours ago. It was possible he was no longer at Mount Prince.

She leaned forward and added another piece of wood to the fire. Justin peeled his gloves off and looked down at his hands. They were bright red.

"Emelia may have faked her pregnancy, but I don't think she faked her belief that her son had been taken. I don't know enough to diagnose her with anything, but she really seemed convinced Matty was gone. It reminded me of the way Sadie could get when she was having a drug overdose. She'd hallucinate and have delusions that seemed so real to her. Drugs can also cause weakness, shakiness and weight loss. But I just don't see any evidence that Emelia suffers from addiction."

"Right now, I've got facts and I've got feelings." Violet gestured to the floor on one side of her and then the other, as if she'd put both in separate piles. "It's like they're pieces to two different puzzles, and I don't know how they fit together."

She leaned back against the couch.

"Imagine you'd never met any of the people in this case," she went on, "and I told you I've got a situation where there's a woman, her husband and her nanny all living in the same house. Husband and wife sleep in separate rooms. The wife gets up in the night and finds the husband missing and the nanny's door locked. What's the first conclusion you jump to?"

"That there was something going on between the father and the nanny."

"Right." Violet stretched her legs and stood. "But I don't think that's the case, because Ariel seems deeply devoted to her friendship with Emelia and doesn't think much of Frank." Violet started pacing behind the couch. Justin turned his head to watch her. "I know the only thing that matters is that we get close enough to one of our three suspects, Matty himself or the cottage to get something with his DNA on it. But I'd still like something about this case to make sense."

Violet stopped pacing and sat on the arm of the couch.

Justin stayed on the floor leaning back against the couch, with his feet stretched out toward the fireplace, so they were at right angles to each other like a clock whose hands were stuck at twelve and three.

"I can believe that Emelia either got pregnant and miscarried or that she mistakenly thought she was pregnant," Violet went on. "I can believe she faked her pregnancy to keep Frank from leaving her and even that she somehow convinced Ariel to help her. What I can't understand is how Frank fits into all this. Because I can't imagine Emelia finding the L.B. Syndicate all on her own without help. Or that Frank would be foolish enough to hang out at this camp playing happy family for three long weeks after buying somebody else's stolen child. We're missing something, and I don't know what it is. All I know is I'm not going to figure it out tonight."

Justin slowly unzipped his coat and eased himself out of the sleeves.

"Go try and get some sleep. I don't know if things will look any clearer in the morning, but lack of sleep won't make it any better. Also, I packed some granola bars and trail mix in the front pocket of the rucksack with the baby gear in case you're hungry." He glanced back at her over his shoulder. His smile looked tired but genuine. "If I'm right in thinking you like granola bars and trail mix?"

"Yes, I do. Thank you. Also, for what it's worth, I'm sorry I never told you about the pizza."

"No worries. Considering everything else I was dealing with at the time, I didn't exactly have time to spend hours researching who made the best Hawaiian pizza in town."

"But you would've tried."

"Yeah."

She chuckled. So did he. Then she felt her smile fade.

"What were you dealing with at the time?" she asked. "I could tell you were worried and weighed down, and I'm wishing I'd asked what all you were dealing with."

Justin turned and faced the fire. Shadows from the flames danced on his face.

"Even if you'd asked, I don't know if I would've told you," he said. "I've never exactly been good at asking for help. Basically, my sister was getting into constant fights with a social worker at a halfway house she was staying at and wanted me to referee. My brother owed money to a friend and somehow I ended up in the middle of that. My mom was in a panic about which relatives were coming to the wedding. On top of all that I was working double shifts to cover for a colleague of mine who kept dropping the ball, when the team was short-staffed as it was."

"Why didn't you tell me?" she asked. "I had no idea you were working double shifts to cover for someone. And why didn't you let your family figure their own stuff out without putting you in the middle?"

"I don't know," Justin said. "It was like I was in the middle of a hurricane with a thousand things swirling around me and didn't have time to stop and figure out which way was up. I just kept reacting."

She'd always known Justin was a caring man—and she admired his heart so much—but was that really how he saw his place in the world? To stand in the hurricane and keep everybody's else's lives from falling apart? No wonder he hadn't been ready to marry her.

"But why didn't you just take a deep breath and hit Pause?" she asked.

His eyes snapped to face her again.

"Because I was worried that if I did, something would go terribly wrong," he admitted. "And I was right. Sadie asked me to adopt Matty. I told her I needed time to think about it, and less than twenty minutes later he was kidnapped."

"That wasn't your fault," Violet said.

"How do you know?" he asked. "Maybe if I'd reacted differently, stayed there with Sadie and talked things out a few minutes longer, Matty would have never been kidnapped. Maybe I wouldn't be sitting here in this cabin knowing that my nephew is now lying in a crib in the home of the family who bought him from his kidnappers."

"Or maybe they'd have kidnapped Matty later that night after you left for work. Maybe they would've kidnapped a different child, and we'd have no idea where to find them."

Didn't he realize that if he spent his life worrying over what would happen if he wasn't there to save the day, he'd drive himself crazy with guilt over things that were out of his control?

Then she watched as his sad eyes searched the flames and realized that maybe he already did.

Justin's phone buzzed soon afterward letting them know it was three in the morning and the time they'd planned to switch rooms. She went into the bedroom, pulled a mattress off one of the bunks and dragged it into the living room so Justin would have something other than the couch to sleep on. Then she wished him goodnight, went into the bedroom and shut the door, noticing Justin had put one of his portable, sliding backup locks on that door, too. She plugged her phone into an outlet under the window, set the alarm for eight and lay down on the bunk opposite the one Justin had slept on.

Despite the exhaustion that radiated through her limbs, Violet didn't expect to fall asleep. She hadn't even realized she had until she awoke to hear the triangle clanging and see a sliver of bright light beaming through the cracks in the shutters. She got up and pulled the shutters back. Blinding morning sunlight filled her gaze. The rain that had fallen in the night had frozen into a dazzling sheet of ice that coated the ground and encased each tree branch, twig and pine needle. She reached for her phone. It was dead.

"Violet?" Justin knocked on her door.

"I'm sorry I overslept," she called. "My phone is dead."

"It's not just you," Justin said. "My phone is dead, too. It looks like the power is out in the entire camp. Thankfully, I've got a portable battery charger, but I doubt we'd get much of a cell signal anyway."

Violet quickly changed her sweater, splashed water on her face and ran a brush through her hair. She plugged their phones into Justin's portable charger and tucked them both inside her jacket pocket. Then she and Justin set out for the lodge.

The ice was so thick their feet skidded across the surface without making a dent. She couldn't imagine how treacherous the narrow mountain road out of the camp would be. As they approached the lodge, they could hear the sound of raised voices coming from inside. It sounded like Don, and maybe others, were arguing.

She glanced at Justin, and his eyebrows rose. But before they could figure out what the ruckus was about, she noticed Ariel slip out of the side door and head toward the path which led to the DuBois cottage.

"Hey!" Violet called and hurried toward her. "How are you doing? Some storm last night, huh?"

Ariel turned back. She had a large, covered tray of what Violet guessed was food in her hands.

"Good morning," Ariel said. The smile that crossed Ariel's face seemed genuine but still Violet could see the worry in her eyes. "Yeah, power is out for the entire camp. Thankfully, the kitchen has gas stoves. We do have a backup generator that covers the lodge and some of the primary buildings, but Lorenzo wasn't able to get it working."

"What's all the noise about in the lodge?" Violet asked.

Ariel took a step back toward the tree line as Violet and Justin reached her. Ariel lowered her voice.

"Some of the investors say they've seen enough and want to head home. Ross is trying to convince them to stay until tomorrow." She sighed. "Lorenzo had tried to tell him that the camp wasn't ready for this kind of investor weekend. But when Ross found out Frank, Emelia and I were leaving, he wanted to quickly throw something together for potential investors while we still had enough staff to run it." She turned to Justin. "We haven't actually met. Are you Viv's husband?"

"I am," Justin said. "I'm Josh. Nice to meet you."

"Nice to meet you, too," Ariel said. "You're the one who lent Emelia your coat last night, right? That was really nice of you."

"No worries. How is she feeling today?"

"She's okay."

Violet could tell Ariel didn't really believe what she was saying. "Is that her breakfast?"

"Yeah," Ariel said. "Emelia wasn't feeling up to coming to the lodge for breakfast today. Her stomach doesn't always like camp food. Hopefully, it'll be better for her in Europe. Frank used to give her this special Scandinavian hot chocolate, and it really helped her sleep. He gave me some for Christmas, too."

Something in her tone made Violet wonder if she was trying to convince them that Frank was a good person. Or maybe convince herself. She couldn't imagine the tone had been all that comfortable in the cottage last night.

"You mentioned she'd been sick a lot," Violet said, "and Lorenzo didn't seem to think Matty was really missing. I don't want to pry, but Josh has had some experience dealing with addiction—"

"Addiction?" Ariel's voice rose. "You mean you think Emelia drinks or takes drugs? No, nothing like that. She's just really delicate. Well, according to Frank."

"Emelia told us that Frank was missing last night, and when she tried to knock on your door, it was locked."

Violet wondered if she was taking a risk asking about something so potentially personal. But Ariel just frowned.

"Yeah," Ariel said. "I usually wake up whenever Matty cries. I can't believe I slept through it." The sound of a walkie-talkie crackled from Ariel's pocket. She pulled it out and held it to her ear. "Okay, yeah, one minute." She put it back in her pocket. "That was Lorenzo. I've got to drop this food off and then get to the rock-climbing cliffs. Lorenzo wants me to get there early to check the harnesses. Should be a lot of fun, and I hope you guys will be there. Then I've got to rush back and finish packing before we leave."

"You're going at the end of the week, right?" Violet asked.

Ariel shook her head. "Not anymore. Frank told me this morning he managed to rent us a private jet at an airfield not far from here. We leave tonight."

SEVEN

Ariel hurried away. Justin turned to Violet, and they locked eyes.

"Tonight. Is it even possible to get a DNA sample to the lab, get it tested and issue a warrant to stop them from leaving the country with Matty by then?"

"It's possible, Justin, but it'll be tight. We're just going to have to be more aggressive about getting Matty's DNA sample, as much as I don't want to risk getting caught. But the moment we know the cabin is empty or see Matty's diaper bag left unattended, we're going to have to go for it."

Justin closed his eyes and silently prayed for help. When he opened his eyes, he saw Violet's head was bowed, too, and heard her whisper, "Amen."

"You good?" she asked.

Determination shone in her gaze. He took a deep breath and felt fresh strength fill his core.

"Yeah." He offered her his hand, she took it and they walked around the lodge and in through the front door.

The first thing he noticed was that one of the investor couples had already packed their bags and left them by the wall inside the door. Food was laid out buffet-style beside the kitchen pass-through. While a few people were milling around with plates, most stood watching Don and Ross, who still seemed locked in whatever conversation they'd overheard when they first approached the lodge.

"Look, I'm not concerned about the fact one of your staff had a medical emergency in the middle of the night," Don said. "Or the fact one of your staff made an inappropriate comment to my wife about it this morning."

Justin wondered who that was and when that had been. Don's arms were crossed, and he looked more frustrated than anything else.

"I fly people into very remote areas for our wilderness tours," Don added, "and I've seen all kinds of medical crises from heart attacks to panic attacks. My concern is that there didn't seem to be any serious contingency plan in place to take care of her."

"I appreciate your concern about a member of our staff," Ross said. "Believe me, I care deeply about every member of the Mount Prince Wilderness Resort family. But I assure you it was a minor and private incident."

"With all due respect, you're missing Don's point," Scott chimed in. He looked around at the others. "I know I'm not in the same line of work as you all. But we do a lot of wilderness training in the reserves. Personally, I don't care that the beds are uncomfortable, there are rat traps in the cabins, the water is freezing cold or the power is out. But I've had the feeling something was off about this place since yesterday, and I think we all just want to make sure people are safe."

Was it his imagination or did Scott's eyes flicker in Justin's direction when he said something felt off? Did Scott think there was something off about him?

"Do you have any idea when the power will be back on?" Gloria asked.

"Lorenzo's working on it now," Ross said. "I'm sure it won't be much longer. Then we've got a whole day of activities planned, including rock climbing, skating and a cedar plank barbecue."

"Thank you, but we've seen enough to know that we're not interested in investing in your camp at this time," Missy said. Her tone was calmer than her husband's had been, but also sounded more final. "While we appreciate your time and your hospitality, we'd like it if you could drive us back to our vehicle as soon as possible."

"We feel the same," Toby added. "We have dinner with the grandchildren every Saturday night and are eager to get back home for it." He gestured to the bags stacked by the door, and Justin wondered when they'd made the decision to leave. "But we do agree this place has some strong potential, so Carol and I would be happy to consider coming up another weekend in the future when you've got a stronger pitch in place to address the issues we've raised. I'm sure many of the others feel the same way."

"I see." Ross's perpetual salesman's smile faded. "Are any of you planning on staying for the rest of the weekend? Or should I ask Lorenzo to stop working on the generator and focus on shuttling people back to the parking lot?"

Ross glanced around the circle.

Justin started to pray that he and Violet wouldn't be the only two who decided to stay. Otherwise, it would be even harder to get Matty's DNA. He watched as Scott whispered something to Gloria and Missy said something to Don.

"Scott and I will stay," Gloria said. "Our flight home doesn't leave until tomorrow, and I'd like to get a wider breadth of what the camp has to offer even if we're not ready to invest at this time."

Justin silently thanked God.

"We're happy to stay until tomorrow, too," Justin said. "Viv and I really love climbing and did it a lot when we were dating. I don't think Dukes Wilderness Adventures is ready to invest, but it would be good to see more."

"And Missy and I aren't in a rush," Don added. "And we still have to pack up if you want to take the Whitchers first."

Ross quickly acknowledged what they'd all said, before switching back to his regular platitudes about how great his camp was, trying to squeeze in every last moment of sales pitch that he could.

Justin signaled Violet, and they moved over to the closest table.

"I think we should grab food quickly," he said softly, "head to the climbing hill and try to talk to Ariel before the others get there. Let's see if we can find out when their cottage will be empty or they'll be bringing Matty to the lodge."

"Agreed. Do you remember how to get there?"

"One Minute" Survey

You get up to **FOUR** books <u>and</u> a Mystery Gift…

ABSOLUTELY FREE!

Romance

YOU pick your books – WE pay for everything!

Suspense

See inside for details.

YOU pick your books –
WE pay for everything.

You get up to FOUR new books and a Mystery Gift…
absolutely FREE!

Total retail value: Over $20!

Dear Reader,

Your opinions are important to us. So if you'll participate in our fast and free "One Minute" Survey, YOU can pick up to four wonderful books that WE pay for when you try the Harlequin Reader Service!

As a leading publisher of women's fiction, we'd love to hear from you. That's why we promise to reward you for completing our survey.

IMPORTANT: Please complete the survey and return it. We'll send your Free Books and a Free Mystery Gift right away. And we pay for shipping and handling too! *We pay for EVERYTHING!*

Try **Love Inspired® Romance Larger-Print** and get 2 books and fall in love with inspirational romances that take you on an uplifting journey of faith, forgiveness and hope.

Try **Love Inspired® Suspense Larger-Print** and get 2 books where courage and optimism unite in stories of faith and love in the face of danger.

Or TRY BOTH!

Thank you again for participating in our "One Minute" Survey. It really takes just a minute (or less) to complete the survey… and your free books and gift will be well worth it!

If you continue with your subscription, you can look forward to curated monthly shipments of brand-new books from your selected series, always at a discount off the cover price! Plus you can cancel any time. So don't miss out, return your One Minute Survey today to get your Free books.

Pam Powers

"Yeah." Justin nodded. "I paid pretty close attention to the layout of this place yesterday."

As much as he hated the idea of trying to sneak into the cabin in daylight or grabbing something from the diaper bag in a public place, they were running out of options and time.

They hung around the lodge for a few more minutes, making small talk and eating some, then as breakfast began to wrap up, Justin and Violet took the usual way back to the cabins until they were out of view. He gestured to a narrow path through the trees. They cut through and came out on one of the marked paths they'd walked on their tour the day before. They turned south and continued until they reached a fork in the path.

"This way," Justin said.

A sudden scream—terrified and panicked—filled the air.

They ran down the icy path toward the sound. The trees parted. A steep drop-off from the cliffs lay ahead of them, with a small wooden hut for climbing equipment.

Ariel stumbled out of the trees so quickly he wondered if some unseen person had shoved her. Justin forced his legs to run after Ariel, with Violet matching pace beside him.

"Ariel!" Violet called. "Are you okay?"

She didn't seem to hear them. Ariel staggered unsteadily as if injured or drunk.

"Ariel!" he shouted. "What happened? What's wrong?"

But it was like whatever had happened to make her scream had also left her so disoriented she could barely register what was going on around her. She stumbled forward.

"Stop!" Justin ran faster.

But he watched helplessly as Ariel lost her footing, slipped and fell over the edge of the towering cliff down onto the harsh rocks below.

Ariel let out a scream as she disappeared from view. For a long, agonizing second it seemed to hang in the air. Then it fell silent. Justin heard a painful gasp slip through Violet's lips, and he realized she'd stopped running just as suddenly as if someone had punched her in the gut.

"Come on." Justin grabbed her hand and pulled her forward. "Ariel needs us."

They pushed forward toward the ledge. His eyes scanned the forest where Ariel had emerged. There was no one there, but it looked like two sets of footprints scuffed the ground, and he thought he could hear what sounded like someone running away through the trees.

"What happened?" Violet asked.

"I have no idea." Justin said. "Someone probably attacked her with something that left her disoriented. I think they wanted her to fall and for it to look like an accident."

They reached the edge of the cliff and looked down. It was a five-story fall of sheer straight rock. Ariel lay at the bottom. Her eyes were closed, and she was on her back like a child's toy that had been tossed on the floor.

He reached for his pocket before realizing Violet was

charging both phones in her pocket. She pulled out his phone and handed it to him.

"No signal," he said. "How about you?"

"No," she said, "but Ariel should have a walkie-talkie, remember?"

He looked back at the climbing equipment hut.

"I'm going to rappel down there," Justin said. "It'll be faster than running back to the lodge, and we still might be able to save her."

He turned to go, but Violet's hand grabbed his arm.

"I'm going with you," she said. "We'll do a tandem climb, like we've done before."

"No," Justin said, automatically. "We'll both be safer if you stay up here and you belay my rope."

"Not if whoever just attacked Ariel comes back and attacks me while you're hanging off the edge of a cliff," Violet said.

Well, it was hard to argue with that.

"Good point. We do this together."

They ran to the equipment shed, and thankfully, it was well stocked. They quickly stepped into harnesses and tightened the buckles. They strapped metal crampons, which would dig like spikes into the ice, to their boots and grabbed curved ice axes that they'd drive into the cliff as they climbed down, both of which would give them a far better grip than they'd get with just their hands and feet alone. Justin and Violet tethered themselves together.

They started rappelling down the cliff. Justin went first, slowly searching for handholds and toeholds in the ice-covered rock. When he was about six feet down, he anchored his ice ax and crampons firmly in the rock and looked up.

Violet was looking down at him.

"All good," he called with what he hoped was a reassuring smile. "Your turn."

"On my way."

He watched as Violet swung her graceful legs over the edge and began to climb down. She was so incredibly strong and moved with such determination it took his breath away. Maybe even intimidated him a little. She passed the place where he now clung to the wall and continued down a few feet. Then she secured herself against the cliff and called up for him to resume his descent. They continued down, taking turns, with one of them always providing stability for the other.

He was anchored about thirty feet from the bottom when he suddenly heard something crack, heard Violet shout and felt her full weight fall into his rope, nearly yanking him clear off the cliff.

Justin gritted his teeth and prayed. He clung to the wall with all four limbs, as his muscles protested in pain and Violet swung like a pendulum on their shared rope while she struggled to regain her grip.

Lord, help me be strong enough to hold on for both of us. Keep me from letting her fall.

Then, mercifully, he felt the rope go slack again.

"I'm good." Violet's voice was breathless "I'm so incredibly sorry. The rock I was standing on gave way beneath me."

"No problem. Let me know when you're good."

"I'm good."

Thank You, God. He breathed a prayer of thanksgiving under his breath and climbed down after her.

Moments later, they hit the ground, unclipped their harnesses and ran across the ground to where Ariel lay. Violet knelt down beside the fallen woman and brushed the dark hair from her face.

"She's not breathing," Violet said, "and I can't find a pulse."

She pulled the walkie-talkie from Ariel's pocket and handed it to Justin. He switched it on, and she started CPR.

"Break, break!" Justin called. "I have an emergency message. Do you copy? Over."

"Copy, this is Lorenzo," the operations chief responded.

"We need search and rescue," Justin said. "Ariel fell over the cliff beside the rock-climbing hut."

Lorenzo gasped a breath. "Copy."

Justin heard Lorenzo shout to somebody else to call search and rescue. Seconds later a male voice called something back to him. Then Lorenzo's voice returned, sounding shakier than it had before.

"Search and rescue are on their way," Lorenzo called. "Who am I talking to? What's going on?"

"It's Josh," Justin called. "There was an accident and Ariel fell. We climbed down to her, and we're with her now."

"Is she breathing?"

"I don't know."

"I'm on my way!"

"Copy that," Justin said.

He ended the call and ran over to Violet.

"How can I help?"

"Take over the compressions. I'll do the breathing. You do the count."

He dropped to the rock beside her and they started working in tandem.

Please, Lord. Please save her life.

Then he heard Ariel shudder a breath. He sat back. Violet cradled the woman's head into her hands. And he watched as tears of relief flooded Violet's eyes.

"Ariel," Violet said, gently. "Can you hear me? It's Viv and Josh. You had an accident."

Ariel groaned slightly. Her eyes fluttered open and then closed again. Her arms twitched as if she was trying to sit up.

"Don't move," Violet said. "Search and rescue are on their way. Can you tell me what happened?"

A faint and sickly-sweet smell reached Justin's nose, but he couldn't place it.

Ariel's eyes opened again. Her pupils were wide, and her gaze was vacant.

"We heard you scream," Violet said. "Did someone attack you? Do you know who it was?"

Please, Lord, help us get some answers.

"Little Blossoms." Ariel's voice was so weak he could barely make out the words. "Warn…Emelia…about… Little Blossoms. Warn her."

"Little Blossoms?" Justin repeated. As in L.B Syndicate. "Who's that?"

"They…got… Matty."

"They took Matty? Or they got Matty for Emelia?" Violet glanced at Justin. Then Violet took a deep breath.

"Is Matty adopted?" Violet's voice was urgent. "Was he adopted from Little Blossoms? Did Emelia and Frank tell you to keep it a secret?"

Fear flooded Ariel's face. Her body jerked up so suddenly that Viv had to try to ease her back down.

"Frank doesn't know about Matty!" Ariel's voice rose. "Emelia says Frank can't know! Please, you have to warn Emelia to protect Matty."

"Frank doesn't know that Emelia adopted Matty from Little Blossoms?" Violet asked. But how did that square with what they knew? "Lorenzo said you'd said something about how having a baby would help Frank get his inheritance."

"No, no, no, it has to be a secret…" Ariel's head shook. "Frank can't know. Nobody knows. We deleted everything."

Did that mean they'd found Little Blossoms online? Ariel was disoriented and babbling, Justin thought. In a similar way to how they'd found Emelia the night before. He wasn't even sure Ariel knew where she was and what she was saying. But she was clearly terrified.

"It's okay," Justin said. "It's going to be okay. We'll keep Matty safe."

"No!" Ariel said. "I can't tell you! You can't know. Or they'll kill Matty!"

EIGHT

"Who will kill Matty, Ariel?" Violet asked. "Little Blossoms?"

She could feel fear building inside her and battled to keep it at bay. She remembered what Anthony had told her about how the other baby's family had been found dead. Had Ariel been attacked and her attempted murder staged as an accident because she knew about Matty? Was she targeted because she'd talked to Violet?

The roar of a snowmobile filled the air, and she could hear Lorenzo shouting. Justin stood. So did Violet.

"Ariel!" Lorenzo shouted. "Josh! Viv! Where are you?"

"Down here!" Josh called.

A yellow emergency rope ladder tumbled over the side of the cliff. Seconds later, they saw Lorenzo climbing down it so quickly his feet barely touched the rungs. "Is she okay? Is she breathing? Is she conscious?"

He leaped off the ladder and ran toward them. Violet met him a few feet away from Ariel.

"She's in and out of consciousness," Violet said. "But she seems stable for now."

Lorenzo's eyes rose to the sky.

"Thank you!" he expelled the words in a single breath so forcefully that Violet wondered if he was praying. Lorenzo dropped to the ground beside Ariel.

A faint sound rumbled in the distance. Violet pulled Justin aside.

"That might be the helicopter," Violet whispered. "Cover for me. I want to try and contact Anthony. I know there's no signal, but I have to try."

Justin nodded. Then without missing a beat, he strode over to join Lorenzo and asked him where the closest search and rescue dispatch was based.

Violet silently thanked God for partnering her with someone who was so unflappable and reliable in an emergency.

Then she walked a few steps away and pulled her phone out of her pocket. The signal had half a bar. She prayed and then typed.

Ariel was attacked. Didn't see it. Seemed disoriented. Fell over cliff. Search and rescue incoming. Keep her secure. Investigate Little Blossoms.

The icon spun, telling her the phone was trying to send the message. All it needed was to catch a signal for just a fraction of a second and it would go through. The message failed. She tried again.

A second person started down the rope ladder. She looked up. It was Scott. A chorus of worried voices filled the cliffside above her. Faces peered over. As much as it pained her inner cop to know they might be trampling over evidence, she also knew there was no way to secure the scene without blowing her cover.

The roar of the helicopter grew closer. Scott joined Lorenzo by Ariel's side and started checking her vitals. Scott was a Canadian ranger, and Violet knew his first aid training would be second to none. Within moments a yellow search and rescue helicopter hovered above them, shaking the trees and sending ice crystals falling. Two Canadian armed service paramedics in bright orange jumpsuits dropped down from above. Justin ran to the nearest one and briefed him quickly on how they'd seen her fall over the cliff and their attempt to keep her alive until rescue got there.

Then Justin joined Violet and put an arm around her shoulder, as search and rescue made their way to Ariel. She leaned her head into the crook of his neck so they could try to talk without being overheard. The warmth of his body seemed to radiate through her core. The smell of him filled her sense, reminding her of safety and home.

"Search and rescue say they'll get her to the hospital in less than thirty minutes and will have the ER prepped for her arrival," Justin said.

Violet breathed a prayer of relief. Then she glanced at her phone and hope leaped in her heart.

"I think my text got through," she called into his ear.

The stretcher rose into the sky with Ariel strapped to it. The paramedics rose, too, and then the helicopter took off again. Violet prayed for Ariel's safety. It wasn't until the helicopter had disappeared over the horizon that she realized she hadn't pulled away from Justin's arm, and he hadn't let go of her, either.

"We need to get back to the cabin and try to get in touch with Anthony," she said, keeping her voice low enough they wouldn't be overheard. "He has to brief whatever medical facility she's taken to and make sure there's security on her door."

Then she glanced at Scott and Lorenzo, who were still standing by the spot where Ariel had fallen. Scott slapped Lorenzo's shoulder like he was trying to reassure him that Ariel would be okay. Then they headed for the rope ladder. Scott ascended first. Then Lorenzo turned to Justin and Violet.

"You guys go ahead," Lorenzo called. "I'll anchor it and keep it steady."

"Thank you," Violet said.

Lorenzo's face was so white he looked sick. The worry that pooled in his eyes was so deep they almost looked hollow. And although Violet knew that duplicitous people knew how to fake their feelings, the depth of his concern for his coworker looked genuine. She patted his arm.

"It's going to be okay," she said. "She's conscious and breathing steadily, and the paramedics will take care of her."

Lorenzo swallowed hard. "I'm going to take a camp vehicle and follow her to the hospital so she has someone there when she wakes up."

"I'm sure she'd appreciate that."

Violet gathered up her climbing gear, slung it over her shoulder and started up the ladder. The wind whipped against her body. The thin plastic rungs shook beneath her feet. And although her brain knew that climbing a rope ladder was a whole lot safer then free-scaling down the cliff with Justin, somehow it didn't feel that way.

As she reached the top, an unfamiliar, bearded man in his midtwenties glanced down at her. The white circular badge on his orange jacket told her that he was a local search and rescue civilian volunteer, the kind that often came to lend a helping hand in an emergency.

"Everybody stand back!" he shouted. "Don't worry, darling! My name's Brent and I've got you!"

It took Violet's brain half a second to click that she was the "darling" this stranger was talking to.

"Thanks," she called. "I'm fine."

But as Brent's fingers grasped the top rung, he reached for her forearm arm, apparently intent on helping her up the last final few steps.

"I got you," he said, again. "Upsy-daisy. Just a few more steps now."

"I told you, I'm fine."

But he had reached for her other hand as well. And as she stood, he tried to guide her away from the ledge as if she was an elderly Victorian lady being led away from her carriage.

"There you go," Brent said. "Safe and sound."

Scott, Gloria, Ross, the rest of the staff and another civilian volunteer gathered around them, watching. Don and Missy were there, too, evidently not having left the camp before the call came in about Ariel's fall. Don was standing closest to the edge, a bit in front of the others, and Violet guessed he'd decided to stay up top and manage the perimeter instead of climbing down, in which case they had him to thank for the fact twenty people hadn't tried to join them. Only then did she notice Frank, standing at the very back of the group, without Emelia or Matty, just watching.

Quite the audience. She gritted her teeth and wondered if it would help or hurt her cover-identity if she snapped in Brent's patronizing face and told him she didn't need saving. She looked back. Justin had started up the ladder.

But when she looked up, Brent was staring at her intently.

"Wait, I know you," Brent said. "I never forget a face. We've met somewhere before. Haven't we?"

A warning bell sounded at the back of her mind. She racked her mind for his face and name but came up empty. "I'm pretty sure we've never met."

She glanced back down. Justin was two thirds of his way to the top.

"Oh, wait!" Brent snapped. "I've got it! My buddy had posted about you on his social media, so I looked it up and turned out you were so cute I sent you a friend request, but you didn't respond. Your name begins with a V or something—"

"I automatically delete requests from people I don't know—"

But Brent wasn't even listening. "You're that chick who gave your wedding away to your brother last spring when your lousy, no-good cretin of a fiancé dumped you at the altar on your wedding day!"

Justin froze, suspended on the rope ladder, just two feet away from the top of the ledge as he heard a loud-mouthed stranger announce to a group of potential suspects the biggest regret of his life.

Please, Lord, don't let my mistake jeopardize this case and hurt our ability to rescue my nephew.

He kept climbing.

"Is that true?" Gloria asked. "But your proposal story sounded so romantic."

"Oh yeah," the stranger leaped in before Violet could. "From what I heard, this guy was a real piece of garbage. Trust me, darling, you're better off without him. In fact, if you ever want to grab a coffee—"

"No, my fiancé did not dump me at the altar!" Violet's voice rose. Her tone snapped like a whip through the air. "I don't know where you got your information, but you're wrong, and I'm very happily married."

She ran for Justin as he reached the top of the ladder. He climbed over the top and stood. Violet grabbed his hand and held it.

"Josh, honey, this here is Brent." She gestured to a bearded man in a civilian search and rescue jacket. "Apparently a friend of Brent's was gossiping about our wedding situation online and got their wires crossed."

Justin quickly took in that Scott, Gloria, Frank, Ross and others were standing around them. While some were shuffling their feet and others were diverting their gaze, he knew they were listening and suddenly wondering how much of what Justin and Violet had told them about themselves were true.

"We don't like to talk about our wedding," Violet added, looking around the group, "because it's not a happy story. But we did decide to call off our wedding a few days before it was supposed to happen, because of some personal stuff that people we cared about were going through." She glared at Brent. "Stuff that is nobody's business, and no, I wasn't dumped at the altar."

Brent's face reddened. His mouth opened and shut again, as if preparing to explain to a stranger he'd just unprofessionally hit on during a rescue operation that she was wrong about her own wedding. "Well, my buddy is a friend of your brother, and I heard—"

"That thankfully my brother had recently gotten engaged as well, so we offered to let them buy out our wedding bookings, which they did?" A confident smile crossed her face. "Setting aside for a moment how rude it is to pass judgement on a stranger's life that way, I'm glad I gave my wedding to my brother. I didn't want a big wedding. I'm glad we eloped instead. Because Josh is the most incredible, caring and thoughtful man I know. I didn't need a big wedding or any of that to be happy. I just needed my husband."

A lump formed in Justin's throat.

He wished it was true and that they had eloped.

"Is everything okay?" Lorenzo climbed over the top of the ledge. He stood and scanned the gathered faces, as he rolled up the ladder. "Did I miss something?"

"Viv was just correcting one of the search and rescue volunteers about some gossip concerning her wedding," Scott said.

Ross turned to Lorenzo. "Once you take Don and Missy back to their car, I'd like you to come meet me in my office to discuss what's happened. Also, can you make sure there are hot drinks in the lodge for anyone who needs them?"

"Actually," Lorenzo said, "if it's okay with you, I'd like to drive straight to whatever hospital Ariel is transported to, so that there's someone there for her when she wakes up."

"We can discuss that," Ross said.

Violet turned to Justin. She still hadn't let go of his hand.

"Let's drop our climbing gear in the hut and get back to our cabin."

"Sounds good." Violet pulled away from him as Justin glanced at the others. "We're just going to go get changed and turned around. We'll join you all at the lodge in a bit."

They hurried to the climbing hut before anyone could try to pull them back into a conversation, stashed their equipment away on the hooks and shelves where they'd found it and set off down the path. Justin had the odd feeling that people were watching them go. Violet shuddered and grimaced, as if she'd just tasted something disgusting. Her fists clenched.

"You okay?" Justin kept his voice low enough so that anyone who was watching wouldn't overhear his words.

"I'm angry," Violet muttered. "The nerve of that jerk back there to act that way." He watched as her jaw clenched. "It was bad enough when Scott leaped in to try to 'rescue' me from you last night. But the way Brent was talking about you really made my blood boil."

He wasn't exactly wrong about me.

"Thank you for having my back."

"No problem," Violet said. "When in doubt, stick to the truth."

"That was hardly the truth, though."

Violet stopped walking. She turned to face him, and it was like all the flame that had been burning inside her eyes now fixed their light on his face.

"It's true that you are the most caring and thoughtful man I know," she said, softly. "And I didn't need a big wedding to be happy, I just needed you."

He broke her gaze. They were still being watched.

"You do know he was completely wrong about you," Violet pressed. "Don't you?"

No, I don't know that. And neither do you.

He managed to stop himself from saying the words that crossed his mind. But it was like Violet somehow heard them anyway. She reached up and brushed her hand along the side of his jaw.

"Listen, you have to stop beating yourself up," she whispered. "Yes, you hurt me. Worse than any pain I'd ever known. But you did it because you cared about me and wanted what was best for me. You are the most incredible and caring man I've ever known, and maybe we weren't ready to get married."

"So you forgive me?"

"Of course, I forgive you."

Justin hadn't even realized how much something inside him had longed to hear her say those words, until a wave of emotions crashed over him.

He felt relieved and sad, but also joyful.

He felt forgiven.

Suddenly, he found himself wrapping both of his arms

around her waist and hugging her tightly. She slipped her hands around his neck and hugged him back. And then somehow, instinctively and without even meaning to, he kissed her.

NINE

In that moment, Violet didn't even know if Justin had been the one to kiss her first, or if she'd kissed him, or how their lips had somehow met. All she knew was that in that sweet and fleeting moment, kissing her former fiancé felt as natural and comfortable as taking a breath.

Then he pulled back. So did she, and she watched as Justin glanced back over his shoulder. She followed his gaze. The crowd at the top of the clifftop still hadn't dispersed, and several of them were still looking their way.

Of course. He'd just kissed her to maintain their cover. Nothing more. The moment had been emotional. Their undercover marriage had already been called into question. People might've assumed they were fighting. So it made perfect sense for Justin to drop a quick peck on her lips to keep people from getting suspicious.

But then why had she kissed him back?

They both turned and started walking quickly as if trying to get as far away from the tender moment they'd shared. Search and rescue had told them they'd have Ariel to the hospital in less than half an hour. Violet and

Justin had already spent more time than that climbing up the mountain, dealing with Brent and then getting caught up in a conversation she was already regretting.

Their feet crunched in snow. The kiss had been a mistake. It might've been good for the cover, but it had been bad for her focus. She couldn't let anything like that happen again ever. It was best not to think about it and definitely not talk about it. She had to push it out of her mind and pretend like it had never happened. Although her resolve was almost altered when she glanced at Justin and saw he looked nearly as shocked and confused as she felt.

They were both practically jogging when they reached the cabin. Justin checked the security camera and bolted the door with his portable lock. She made a beeline for the uncomfortable couch, kicking off her boots as she went. Her phone had one bar.

"I'm going to call my brother now, okay?"

Justin nodded. She placed the phone on the coffee table, put it on speakerphone, dialed her brother's number and went through the security check. Finally, she heard her brother answer. "Hello?"

"Hey, bro, it's me." Violet sat on the floor beside the table so the phone was at shoulder height. "I'm here with Justin again, and you're on speaker."

"Gotcha, and I'm here with Tessa. She was able to use her private detective skills to find out more than I could through official channels. But first, I'm guessing you'll want an update on Ariel."

"Please," Violet said.

Justin sat down on the edge of the sofa, on the opposite side of the table, pulled out his laptop and started typing.

"Ariel is alive and arrived at the hospital a few minutes ago," Anthony said. "She's got some broken bones and trauma from the fall. But the main concern is that they rushed her into a CT scan for potential brain trauma and found some very abnormal swelling that doctors can't figure out the source of. They're going to put her in a medically induced coma until the swelling goes down. It's too soon to tell if she'll ever come out of it."

Violet closed her eyes tightly and felt unshed tears rush to the underside of her lids.

"Get a guard on her door and don't let anyone in to see her without authorization," Violet said. "Even her friends."

"Already on it," Anthony said. "What can you tell me about what happened?"

Violet was thankful when Justin launched into the story of what they'd seen, from hearing Ariel scream, to seeing her stumble out of the woods and fall over the cliff.

"We think whoever was behind it staged it to look like an accident," Justin said. "We rappelled down, performed CPR and called for help with her walkie-talkie."

"And she regained consciousness?" Anthony asked.

"She did," Violet said. "She was terrified and only semi-coherent. She seemed to be saying that Frank had no idea that Matty wasn't Emelia's child and that Little Blossoms would kill Matty if Frank or anybody else found out Matty was adopted."

"So she confirmed that Matty was adopted and that Little Blossoms was the name of the adoption agency?" Anthony pushed.

"Not in so many words, but she implied it," Violet said. "And she gave us the name Little Blossoms. Guessing that's what the *L* and *B* in L.B. Syndicate stand for. She wanted us to warn Emelia to protect Matty. But she was really out of it and desperate. Maybe she was concussed. We'd be hard-pressed to get a warrant issued, let alone a criminal conviction, off what she said. Have you found anything on Little Blossoms?"

"Not yet," Anthony said. "All the regular law enforcement channels were a bust."

"And I haven't found anything through unofficial back channels or the dark web," Tessa added.

"I'm searching the dark web now, too," Justin said. "Not much of an internet signal, but I'm making it work for me."

"Anything else?" Anthony asked.

"We almost had our cover blown by some volunteer search and rescue guy named Brent," Justin said and quickly filled him in.

"I'm sorry," Anthony said when Justin had finished relaying the story. "Tessa and I made a specific effort to be discrete and kind in everything we said about your wedding, and to be honest that name doesn't ring a bell, off the top of my head. How about you, Tessa?"

"Already on it," Tessa called. They heard typing in the background. "I think he's the cousin of that awkward guy your friend from college brought as a date when her original date canceled."

Anthony groaned.

"I'm looking at a social media page now," he said. "Yeah, I think that's it. Again, I'm really sorry, guys."

"No problem," Violet said. "It was fine."

Except for the fact she and Justin had gotten into an unexpectedly emotional conversation afterward and ended up kissing.

"Our bigger concern is that, according to Ariel, Frank's hired a private jet and is planning on flying out tonight," Violet added. "That doesn't give us a lot of time to get Matty's DNA. Plus, I expect that soon it's going to get really hard to explain why we haven't left yet."

"If it's any help," Tessa said, "Ranger Scott Danis passed the background check I ran on him with flying colors. He has paramedic training. He was actually hoping to go to medical school. But then his best friend's wife was attacked by a colleague and died. Really tragic story. Turned out the guy was living a double life and had been stalking her. Left behind two little kids. So Scott loaned his widower friend all his savings to help him keep a roof over his kids' heads. Kept the loan a secret, too, because he didn't want the credit. I don't even think his mom knows."

"Wow," Violet said.

Maybe that was why he'd reacted so strongly when he'd mistakenly thought Violet was in trouble. Scott's words to Ross at the awkward dinner the night before filled her mind: *I find it's hard to build trust without honesty and vulnerability. Right now, it feels like you're hiding your flaws. We can't work with you if we don't even know who you are.*

He'd been talking about the camp. But he might as well have been talking about her relationship with Justin.

"I've also discovered his mom, Gloria, got a job as an inner-city trauma nurse to help pay the bills in the early years of her marriage to Scott's father," Tessa added.

"And I just found Little Blossoms," Justin said, triumphantly. "Or at least the remnant of a portal they were using. The original has since been deleted, and the links are all dead. But it's a start. Guys, I'm going to read out an internet address. Take it down and pass it on to Seth. He may be able to find more, until I get out of here."

He rattled off a long string of letters, symbols and numbers.

"What are you looking at?" Tessa asked.

Violet looked at the laptop.

"A black screen with the logo of three yellow flowers and a couple blocks of white text," she said. "It reads, 'Little Blossoms is a private and discrete adoption agency for select and exclusive clients wishing to provide a permanent home for carefully selected and procured children. Complete and absolute privacy and discretion are both required and provided.'"

"They left out the part about all that discretion and privacy being enforced by murdering people," Anthony said, dryly. "Have I mentioned that I wish you'd let us get you out of there?"

"Things are wrapping up here," Justin said. "We only have a tiny window of time before we'll have to leave anyway."

The clang of the triangle sounded in the distance.

"And that's our signal to head to the lodge," Justin added. "We'll be in touch soon. Hopefully to inform you we've got Matty's DNA and are heading out to meet up with you."

"Wait," Tess said. "Before you go. One thing I don't understand is how Emelia found Little Blossoms. I've been searching for illegal adoption agencies on the dark web ever since babies started getting kidnapped, and I couldn't find any record of them online. Now, I'm not as skilled as Justin, but I know a lot more than your average civilian. So how come Emelia found them and I couldn't?"

"Good question," Justin said.

They ended the call, left their cabin and made their way back through the snow to the lodge. Thick clouds had moved in again, blocking out the sun and threatening snow. Seemed that despite the morning's respite the winter storm wasn't completely over yet. The camp had never felt all that full, but now it seemed downright deserted. As they reached the clearing, she felt Justin grab her elbow and point her toward the tree line. She followed his gaze and saw why. Frank, Emelia and baby Matty were heading down the path toward the lodge. Did that mean their cottage would be empty? Violet glanced at Justin and his steadfast gaze met hers.

"It's now or never," he said.

"Yeah, I think so, too. One of us should head to the lodge to make sure they don't run off with Matty."

The frown lines that creased his forehead told her that Justin didn't want her to head off to the cabin alone, but he also knew she was right.

"You go," he said. "I'll go to the lodge. I'll keep a hidden earpiece in my ear and my phone free. I'll also grab a walkie-talkie from the storage room as backup."

"Okay." She took a deep breath.

"Stay safe."

"You, too."

She leaned toward him, instinctively wanting to brush a kiss across his cheek, or even his lips, in goodbye. But instead, she caught herself at the last moment and gave him an awkward half hug. Frank and Emelia disappeared into the lodge. Violet turned and hurried back down the path toward her cabin, then slipped into a thick crop of trees, doubled back and then started through the forest toward the DuBois cottage.

It was slow going at first, as she trudged uphill through thick snow, avoiding the regular paths. Finally, the cottage came into view. Her eyes and ears searched the snowy woods around her for any sign of life. She tried the front door and found it locked. The curtains were drawn, and when she tried the windows, they didn't give. Carefully and slowly, she made her way around to the side of the house. The faint imprint of footprints dotted the uneven ground beneath her feet. Seemed she wasn't the first person to have snuck around the side of the cottage.

A wide window lay ahead. She crouched low and glanced in. It was a small kitchenette and laundry room. Dirty mugs and baby bottles were piled high around a small sink. A basket on the floor by the stacked washer-dryer looked full of dirty laundry. She breathed a prayer of thanksgiving. The window was locked by a piece of wood wedged along the bottom of the sill. She slid a small piece of wire from her lock-picking kit into a gap in the window's insulation and jostled it until the wood popped loose and clattered to the floor.

She plugged an earpiece into her ear, dialed Justin's number and then tucked her phone back into her pocket. She waited a few moments as it rang.

"Hey," Justin said, softly. "How's it going?"

"Got my eyes on some solid DNA sources and the window open. About to head in. How are things looking there?"

"Emelia is still in the lodge with Matty," he whispered. "Frank has stepped out onto the front porch to take a phone call."

"Where are you?"

"Just outside the back door by the wood and garbage cans. Lorenzo has taken Missy and Don down the mountain. Scott, Gloria and the rest of the staff are still here. Still no plan for actually getting the DNA sample down the mountain. We might have to just wait for our turn to get driven back to our truck."

"We'll figure it out." Violet braced both palms against the windowsill and hoisted herself up. She slid through the window and landed on a small, square table. "I'm in."

She heard Justin whisper a prayer for her safety and echoed a silent amen.

Then she took off her warm winter gloves, stuffed them in her pocket and pulled on the pair of plastic evidence gloves. She plucked two half-empty baby bottles off the counter and placed them in separate evidence bags, then pulled a dirty receiving blanket from the laundry and slid it into a third bag.

Footsteps creaked on the floorboards from somewhere within the cabin. She froze. "I don't think I'm alone."

"Get out of there!" Justin whispered.

Carefully, she tucked the evidence bags deep into the hidden pockets of her jacket and did the zipper.

The sound of footsteps grew louder. Whoever else was inside the cabin was drawing closer. She turned back to the window to run. Then she saw it—a set of car keys lay in a basket on the counter.

"Hey!" a male voice sounded behind her.

She looked back in time to see Curly standing in the doorway. He was reaching for his gun, but she wasn't about to give him the opportunity to fire.

Violet turned and sprinted for the window, snatching the car keys off the counter before diving headfirst into the snow.

A bullet sounded behind her. The window exploded in a spray of glass. Justin's voice was in her ear, calling her name.

Violet yanked herself to her feet and took off running through the woods.

The sound of gunfire filled Justin's earpiece, followed by the faintest sound of what he guessed was the same noise echoing like a crack somewhere in the vast, snowy forest ahead of him.

"Violet!" Justin whispered as loudly as he dared. "Are you okay?"

Please, Lord, keep her safe. I need her to be all right.

But no answer came in his earpiece except for the sound of footsteps pounding through the snow, tree branches cracking and Violet's ragged breath. She was running, but from whom? And where was she running to?

"Violet!"

A desperate sort of fear filled his core. He had to help her. He had to make sure she was safe.

"Justin!"

"I'm so glad to hear your voice." Involuntarily, his hand rose to his heart, which felt like it was about to explode in his chest with relief.

"Where are you? I'll come find you."

"I don't know. I'm lost. Curly was in the cabin. He opened fire and I took off running. But I've got what we need. Two dirty bottles and a blanket. I'm now heading west down the side of the mountain. I think I'll find the road, then double back up to the lodge. Also, I stole a pair of car keys from the kitchen counter."

"You did what?"

But before she could answer he heard the plaintive sound of Matty crying. He turned back. Emelia staggered through the back door, with Matty bawling in her arms. His tiny fists waved. Her face looked so pale he thought she was about to pass out.

"Hey, it's okay, you're okay," Justin said, reverting to his go-to response for anyone in distress.

Instinctively, he reached for Matty as his heart ached to take his tiny nephew in his arms and cradle him to his chest.

But Emelia crumpled onto the cement block steps and sat.

"Have you seen Frank? I can't find him."

"I saw him on the front porch. He was on the phone. Come on, it's freezing out here. Let's get you both back inside the lodge."

But Emelia didn't move. Instead, as he watched, tears filled her eyes.

"Hey, are you okay?" Justin crouched beside her. "You can talk to me. I know that you and Ariel were close, and it must've been a really big shock what happened to her. She told me it was important to her that she protects you and Matty. If you know anything about what happened to her that could help her now, you can trust me."

Emelia let out a soft sob. Her thin shoulders shook.

"I… I just need a minute. The lodge is too hot. I was feeling queasy."

She hadn't even acknowledged what he'd said about Ariel.

"Do you want me to help you get to a doctor?"

"Emelia! Honey!" Frank's voice boomed down the hallway. "Where are you?"

Emelia shot to her feet.

"I'm fine!" Emelia told Justin. "I'm just tired. Please, don't tell Frank I said anything. I'm good. Really."

"Justin?" Violet's voice crackled in his ear.

It was like I was in the middle of a hurricane…and didn't have time to stop and figure out which way was up. His words to Violet days earlier filled his mind.

"Emelia!" Frank snapped, impatiently. "Answer me! Now!"

Emelia turned and disappeared back into the lodge.

"I'm here, Frank!" he heard Emelia say. "I just popped outside for some air."

Justin hurried away from the lodge and around to the other side of the woodshed.

"Violet! Are you okay? Where are you?"

"I'm okay," she whispered. "I'm hiding behind a building. I can hear Curly out there somewhere looking for me, but I can't see him."

"What building?"

"Remember those ones we saw down a side road before we reached the lodge? One of those. They're all pretty run-down. But I think this is where Curly has been hiding out. Maybe somebody else, too—"

Her words suddenly stopped before she could finish her thought. Had she been caught? Had Curly found her?

"Hang on." Justin started jogging down the road away from the lodge. "I'm coming your way."

He'd gone a couple of hundred yards before Violet's voice was back in his ear.

"Sorry," she said. "Curly got too close for comfort, and I had to change where I was hiding. There are a couple of SUVs here. Not camp ones. Different ones."

He wasn't sure what to make of that news.

"And I've figured out I have the keys to one of them."

Right, she'd told him she'd stolen a set of car keys.

He gasped a breath, and frosty air filled his lungs. He kept jogging down the mountain road away from the camp. He wanted to tell Violet to wait there for him. But if Curly was searching for her, and she had the DNA samples and she'd found a way out—

"Go," he said, without hesitation. "Get the DNA samples to Anthony. Don't wait for me. The sooner we get the evidence to the lab the sooner we get the warrant we need, and this will all be over."

Even without replying, he could hear hesitation hitch in her breath.

"Don't overthink it," he added, knowing as he said the words that he would have done exactly that. "Curly knows you were in the cabin. Frank's going to figure out his keys are gone. Just get out of here as fast as you can, and I'll cover for you!"

Then before she could answer, he heard a muffled voice shout and the sound of Violet running. A car door slammed. A gunshot rang out. Glass shattered. Then an engine roared, and he heard gravel spinning under tires.

"Okay, I'm in an SUV," Violet said. "Curly took out the back window, but I'm on the road and on my way."

"Is he chasing you?"

"I don't think so," Violet said. "Hang on, I'm going to put you on hold, call Anthony and patch you in on a three-way call. Don't worry, I can do it all using hands-free voice commands."

Justin strained his ears and could hear the distant sound of what he thought was Violet's vehicle fleeing the camp. Thick trees surrounded him on all sides. The sky had grown dark. Snow began to fall again in huge, thick clumps. He looked back. He'd walked so far that he'd lost sight of the lodge, except for the slanted roof peaking above the trees.

"Anthony, hi!" he heard Violet's voice say in his ear. "Good news! I've got the DNA samples, and I'm on my way to you now."

Something cracked in the trees behind him. Then suddenly he was struck across the back of the head by what felt liken a wooden bat, and the hard blow knocked him to the ground. Justin shouted in pain. Stars filled his eyes. He tried to struggle to his knees, but a large figure leaped on his back and tried to force him to the ground. A strong hand clamped something over his face. It was a damp fabric soaked in something sweet.

Chloroform!

Justin thrashed from side to side, trying to free himself from his attacker enough to speak. "Viv!… I've… been…"

Drugged…

TEN

The thick and sickly toxin seeped into Justin's lungs. He struggled desperately, trying to catch a breath of fresh air and bury his face in the snow.

Help! God! I have to stay conscious. I can't pass out.

He heard Violet and Anthony shouting, but their voices seemed to be coming from very far away. Then the earpiece dropped from his ear, and their voices fell silent. His brain began to reel off facts about chloroform as if subconsciously searching for something that would save him. It was an unreliable drug. It all depended on the size of the dose, how big the person was and how much time elapsed. Administer too little and the person would just be drowsy for a couple of hours. Too big a dose and the person would die.

A sudden bout of nausea swept over him. His body went limp, and his attacker jumped off it, apparently believing he'd succeeded in knocking him out. Then Justin's attacker grabbed him by the ankles and dragged him along the ground. Frozen rocks and brush scraped his body, and he was thankful to the cold and pain for keeping him conscious. Justin's hands searched the ground for a weapon. His fingers clamped around a large, jagged stone. He didn't know where his attacker was taking him, and he wasn't about to wait to find out.

He gasped a deep breath, summoned all his strength and kicked back hard. The attacker lost his grip, and Justin's leg broke lose. The figure lunged for him again. A masked face filled Justin's view. Justin smashed the rock as hard as he could against the man's right knee. He grunted and fell back. Justin stumbled to his feet and ran blindly down the slippery road.

A horn blared. Headlights cut through the falling snow, blinding his gaze. A silver SUV was flying up the road toward him. And he was right in its path. He threw himself into the snowbank as the vehicle swerved. A snowmobile sounded in the trees. His assailant was getting away. The SUV's door swung open. A figure leaped out.

"Justin!"

His hands raised in self-defense.

"Hey, it's okay!" Violet's voice reached in through the haze of drugs and pain. Then a gentle hand brushed the side of his face. "It's me. You're safe."

He blinked up at her. Violet's beautiful face swam in front of him like a mirage, surrounded by the falling snow and backlit by bright headlights.

"Violet. You came back for me."

"Of course, I did!" She laughed softly, and the sound was music to his ears. "I'm just sorry that whoever did this to you got away. Did you see who it was?"

Justin shook his head. "Masked."

His words felt heavy and sluggish on his tongue, as if he had to push each one through a haze of heavy fog.

"Are you hurt?"

"Drug…ged." He shook his head even though every inch of his body seemed to ache. "Chlo…ro…form."

Violet whispered a prayer under her breath.

"Can you walk?"

He nodded, hoping that he could.

Her arm slid under his shoulders. She helped him to his feet and led him across the ground into the passenger seat of the vehicle. Then she leaned past him to buckle him into his seat belt, and the soft gentle smell of her filled his senses for a moment, ridding the ugly scent of the toxin from his lungs. She closed his door and he slumped against it and closed his eyes. When he opened them again, she was behind the wheel, and they were driving down the road away from Mount Prince.

"Anthony's not exactly happy I went back for you," Violet was saying, and he wondered how long she'd been talking. "We kind of got into it and argued a bit. Not that he doesn't think you're the best, but because he was worried about losing the DNA samples and our best shot at getting a warrant to rescue Matty."

Yeah, Justin was worried about that, too.

"Of course, he didn't realize how much danger you were in. To be fair he was already annoyed at me for taking whoever's SUV this is. Until I explained I was being shot at. I'm sure if I hadn't taken it and gotten shot, my big brother would've reprimanded me for that, too."

She laughed, and he could tell she was trying to keep her voice upbeat and positive. Snow and trees flew past his window. His body jostled from side to side as she drove down the icy mountain road. He was certain she was speeding until he glanced at the bright white speedometer numbers and realized she was probably going slower than he would've.

"But don't worry," she went on. "Because you're going to be fine. You're strong, and I don't think you were hit with that big a dose. You can nap on the way to the lab, and when you've got your wits about you again you can tell me what happened. Do you have any idea who it was that attacked you?"

Justin shook his head, and his eyesight blurred.

"We'll meet up with Anthony and Tessa, get the items in my coat tested for Matty's DNA and wrap this up in no time. I am trying to call Anthony, but I can't get through. He just texted that something was up, and he'd call me back in a moment."

Through the pelting snow a figure caught his eye high on a mountain slope ahead of them. He was crouched low, and Justin wondered for a moment if it was the same man who'd attacked him. But he wasn't sure if his attacker would've been able to make it up there so quickly.

"There's someone—" he started.

The figure disappeared behind a sudden flash of light. A boom shook the sky like a hundred thunderclaps going off at once. The cliffside roared as a gigantic sheet of rock and snow broke off and poured down onto the road ahead of them.

It was an avalanche, and it was heading straight for them.

* * *

"Save us, Lord!" Violet prayed as she hit the brakes and tried to steer the vehicle away from the torrent of falling rocks and snow that roared down the mountain. The tires locked. The vehicle spun. For a moment all she could do was grip the steering wheel and pray as they whirled helplessly, caught between the snow and rock that cascaded toward them on one side and the edge of the cliff that plunged hundreds of feet down on the other. Debris pelted down around the vehicle, clanging on the roof and pouring through the cracked rear window, filling the back seat. With a bone-jarring jolt, the rear bumper slammed into something she couldn't see, and the vehicle stopped. But still the deafening roar of the avalanche filled the car as the onslaught continued.

Until finally it ended. The mountain seemed to rumble beneath her, which she assumed was the sound of whatever debris had managed to cross the road, continuing its way down the mountain. Snow was piled up so high on her side of the car that all she could see was a wall of gray. But a faint sliver of light still trickled in through Justin's side of the vehicle.

"You okay? Looks like we're digging ourselves out on your side."

No response. Justin's face was turned to the window.

"Justin!" Her voice rose as she undid her seat belt and reached for him. His eyes were closed, but when she pulled her gloves off and ran her fingers along his neck, she found that, thankfully, his pulse was still strong. His breaths were shallow and ragged. She cupped his face in her hands. "Listen to me. I need you to wake up and open your eyes for me, babe. I know that you're battling a pretty strong drug that's trying to pull you back to sleep. But I need you right now."

His eyelids flickered but didn't open.

"I'm trying to wake up, but I can't."

Her heart lurched. She could tell he was struggling, and she couldn't imagine how terrifying it must be to try to wake up but keep falling back into unconsciousness.

"Just focus on your breathing and getting more oxygen into your lungs. Big, deep breaths. Nice and slow."

She leaned past him, unlocked his door and tried to push it open. She only managed to get it open half an inch before it wedged in the buildup of snow on the other side. Fresh cold air rushed in. She scooped some snow into her bare hands, cooled her palms and then gently pressed them against his cheeks.

"Thank you. That helps."

The color was returning to his face.

"Now, I need you to take those deep breaths. Just focus on my breath, and we'll do it together." His eyes were still closed. Her mouth was just inches from his lips. She took a deep breath in, held it and then blew it out again. He copied her timing, and she felt the rush of his breath on her face. His breaths began to deepen. Slowly they inhaled and exhaled together, sharing the same air.

Finally, Justin's eyes fluttered open again. But this time they didn't close. Instead, his blue eyes locked on her face. He held her gaze for a long moment. They were so close that if either one of them moved, just a tiny little bit, their lips would touch in another kiss. However, this time there wouldn't be the excuse that they had an audience. And yet, she didn't pull back. Neither did he. Instead, they sat, side by side, in the front seat of the vehicle, with their faces just inches apart.

Did Justin have any idea how much she'd missed him? Yes, she'd forgiven him for calling off the wedding, and she was growing more certain in her belief he'd done the right thing. That didn't change the fact that losing him had felt like losing a part of her own heart. Or that she was struggling to keep her emotional distance from him on this mission.

And Justin would definitely never know just how much something inside her wanted to kiss him right now.

The loud, tinny ring of her cell phone suddenly filled the car. She sat back in her seat and reached for her phone. It was Anthony. But just as she pressed the button to answer the call dropped.

"I doubt I'm going to be able to get a consistent signal until we're out of this snow."

Justin reached into the gap between the door and the frame, scooped a handful of snow out of the way and then pushed on the door again. It opened a couple more inches, with a high-pitched squeak. He undid his seat belt, pivoted on his seat and kicked at the door with both feet. It opened another foot.

He glanced at her. "Can you fit through there?"

"I think so."

He pushed his seat all the way back. Violet put her gloves back on, climbed past him and squeezed through the narrow gap until she was outside the vehicle.

Thankfully, the snow had stopped, but thick, white clouds still blanketed the sky above. Violet looked around and gasped. She was on the camp side of the avalanche. The vehicle's rear was wedged against a huge bolder that had fallen down the mountain. Its front bumper was perilously close to the edge of the cliff, only a few inches away from plunging them straight over the brink to their deaths. A huge mound of snow the size of a small house had landed on the road, blocking their way back down the mountain. Whole trees had fallen over the road, and their huge, twisted roots towered above her.

If the car had been a few feet deeper within the landslide, they might've have been crushed by the weight or suffocated from the lack of oxygen before they made it out alive.

Quickly, she dug Justin's door out the best she could. Then she stood back while he kicked again, and finally it opened enough that he could push his way out.

Justin stumbled from the vehicle, took a couple of steps forward on wobbly legs and then dropped to the ground and sat, with his back against the snow. His head dropped into his hands, and she watched as he gasped for breath.

"Are you okay?" She crouched down beside him.

Her hand reached for him, but he waved her away.

"Give me a moment. I'm really dizzy, and I'm trying not to pass out. Digging our way out like that really took it out of me." He inhaled a long, deep breath. "I can't decide if I should try to walk it off or just sit here for a bit. I don't want to pass out again."

Her phone started ringing. This time she declined the call, stayed crouched on the ground beside Justin and instead texted Anthony that there'd been a hiccup with their plans, and she'd call him back in a moment.

"We need to talk to Anthony, but I want to wait a couple of minutes until you're feeling a little less woozy and a bit more alert. Because I want your mind on this problem, too, and to make sure you're completely on board with whatever solution we come up with. It probably makes the most sense to physically climb over the roadblock and continue down the road on foot. But if you're not up to walking that far, I don't exactly want to leave you here and set off without you. Anthony might be able to drive up and meet us on the other side of this impasse. Or if we go back we might be able to find a snowmobile and take the network of hiking paths Lorenzo had told us about."

"I'm really sorry about all this."

She looked back at him, feeling genuinely confused. "Sorry for what?"

"I'm sorry that I let someone get the jump on me." Justin looked up at her, and sadness pooled in his eyes. His voice sounded less sleepy now but instead like he was annoyed with himself. "I've been going over and over what happened in my mind. I was behind the lodge on the phone with you. Then I started jogging down the road while we were talking. I thought I was alone, then this guy just walloped me with something across the back of my head, like a baseball bat—"

"What?" Violet's voice rose. She leaped to her feet. "You were hit with a bat? You didn't tell me that."

"It might not have been a bat. It could've been a stick or something. I didn't see what it was."

"That's not the point!"

"Anyway, I think he was just trying to get the upper hand so he could drug me. Maybe their end game was to kill me in a way that looked accidental, like what happened to Ariel. I stumbled to the ground. He jumped on me and stuck this piece of cloth soaked in chloroform over my face."

"And you didn't see who it was?"

"No. I'm pretty sure it was a man. He was tall and wearing a mask. I did wallop him pretty hard in his right knee with a rock, so whoever he was, he's probably limping right now." Justin frowned. "And again, I'm sorry. I should've been paying more attention. I didn't even realize somebody had snuck up and gotten the jump on me. And now we're stuck here. I wanted to apologize because I feel like I let you down."

"Don't you dare apologize for being human and getting hurt," she said. His analogy from the night before about feeling like he was trying to stand in a hurricane and save everyone filled her mind. "You are not responsible for every bad thing that happens in the world. Especially not this."

"But if I—"

"You are a police officer who was attacked by a criminal in the line of duty." She cut him off before he could even finish his thought. "Just like countless other people every day. Sometimes when you step up to serve and protect, you put your life in danger. And I'm not going to stand here and let you apologize for that."

Violet started to pace back and forth in front of the crashed wall of snow and debris blocking her off from getting the evidence inside her coat to where it needed to be.

"Maybe the reason it bothers me so much that you hold yourself to an impossible standard, and keep apologizing for not being stronger, is the fact I've spent all my life trying to figure out what standard I should hold myself to," she admitted. "You know how much it bugs me when people just assume I'm helpless and need protection because of who I am and how I look. But, on the flip side, I sometimes feel like..."

Her voice trailed off, sensing she was coming dangerously close to something she'd never really put into words before, let alone told anyone else.

"I feel like people judge me for trying to step up and be strong. And yet, at the same time, I'm worried they'll judge me just as much for being weak. Did you know that almost every first date I've ever been on, the guy has questioned if it's even okay for a woman with a job like mine to get married and have kids? Usually I just brush it off. But then last summer Tessa was abducted while investigating a cold case, and the same criminal nearly killed Anthony, too. It made me think about how fragile and precious life is. We all put our lives on the line every day, and I don't think any of us should apologize for being vulnerable."

"I didn't think of it like that." Justin ran both of his hands through his hair, leaving a smattering of snow in their wake. "I never treated you that way, did I? Or made that kind of comment about your career?"

"No." A smile crossed her lips. "You never did. You've always been one million percent supportive about my career."

Justin exhaled a long breath.

"I was always afraid that if you knew the true extent of everything I was dealing with, you wouldn't have wanted to marry me."

She shrugged. "I guess I always thought we'd handle it together and share the load."

Her phone rang again. It was Anthony.

"I'm going to take this. Good by you?"

"Yeah." Justin stood up slowly.

She walked over to join him, held the phone between them and put it on speakerphone.

"Anthony, hi! Sorry for not answering sooner. Like I said, we've run into a bit of an obstacle."

"You mean the avalanche?" Anthony asked. "Yeah, I was just getting briefed on that. Because it's on private property, the owner, Ross, will be responsible for digging out the road, and that could be months. He's asked search and rescue to send a helicopter to evacuate everyone. But it's not considered an emergency, because nobody was injured or caught up in it, so he's been warned it'll be a few hours."

Evacuation? Was he talking about the same avalanche she was looking at?

"What are you talking about?" Violet said. "I'm looking at the avalanche right now. It's not exactly small, but it won't take people that long to climb over it, if a vehicle drives up to collect them on the other side."

"Violet," Anthony said, "a huge chunk of the mountain split off and crashed down into the parking lot, completely burying the vehicles. The entire lower half of the road is completely gone. Vehicles were crushed. Nobody is driving in or out of that camp until it's rebuilt."

Violet's legs suddenly felt numb.

"Was anybody hurt?"

"No. One of the staff barely escaped being swallowed up in the snow. His name was Lorenzo Segreto and he's the one who called it in. Apparently, he'd driven some guests down, named Don and Missy Kearns. The Kearnses had just gotten into their vehicle and left the property, but when they heard the noise they turned around and came back to make sure everyone was okay. They helped dig him out and have now driven him to the hospital."

"He'll want to see Ariel," Violet said. "He'd mentioned he wanted to have someone there she knew when she woke up. Do you know if she's still in a medically induced coma?"

"She is. They can't risk waking her up until the swelling in her brain goes down, and they still don't know what caused it."

"I think she was chloroformed like I was," Justin said. "I smelled something sweet on her."

"I'll mention that to the hospital," Anthony said. "But I don't think that causes brain swelling."

Violet blew out a hard breath. Neither did she.

"We were just caught up in our own avalanche," she said. "It seems ours was a lot smaller than the one that took out the parking lot. But it blocked the road, and we had to dig ourselves out."

"There was an explosion," Justin added. "I saw somebody on the hill, and he caused the avalanche we're caught up in. I'm guessing there were multiple charges set farther down the hill."

The weight of the DNA evidence Violet was carrying sat heavy in her pockets.

"So our options are to either make our way down to the bottom of the mountain and have you meet us somewhere on the road—which could take a couple hours—or we head back to camp, keep our heads down and wait to be evacuated."

"Looks like it," Anthony said. "I can try to pull some strings and get you an earlier pickup, based on the fact you're carrying potential evidence of a crime."

"But it'll tip your hand immediately if you're the only ones evacuated," Tessa added.

"Agreed," Violet said. "The only consolation is that as long as the road is blocked, Frank, Emelia and Matty are stuck up there, too, and can't flee the country."

Something beeped inside Justin's pocket. He yanked out his phone and stared at the screen.

"Hang on," Justin said. "The motion camera just triggered. Somebody has just broken into our cabin. They must have a staff key."

He held up his phone. Together they looked down at the small black-and-white image that flickered on their screen. Someone was darting around the cabin, carrying a bundle in their arms. She watched as the figure set what they were carrying down on the mattress Justin had left on the floor from the night before, locked the door and then started pushing the couch toward it.

The bundle wriggled. Violet sucked in a sharp breath as her brain suddenly realized what she was seeing.

"It's Emelia," she said. "She's alone with Matty, and she's locked herself in our cabin."

ELEVEN

Uneasiness spread through Violet's core. What was Emelia doing in their cabin with the baby? Why was she alone?

As they watched, Emelia went over to Justin's duffel bag and started dumping his clothes out. Then she stopped suddenly and dropped to the floor behind the couch as if hiding from someone. There was no audio on the camera, but it looked like Matty was fussing.

"We have to go back!" Justin said.

He was right. There was no debate and no argument. Justin's baby nephew was lying on a mattress on the floor in the middle of their cabin, with the woman who'd bought him from kidnappers, and she seemed to be behaving erratically. Emelia stood up again and went back to ransacking Justin's bag.

"Yeah, we've got to go," Violet said.

"Call me when you can," Anthony said, as Violet filled him in. "In the meantime, we're going to drive to the bottom of the mountain so that we're there when you find your way down. As long as you keep your phones on, we can track you by GPS, even if you don't have a cell phone signal."

"And we'll be praying for you," Tessa added.

They ended the call. Then Violet and Justin ran as fast as they could up the winding road back to the camp. Justin's strides were wobbly and uneven, Violet noticed, like his body hadn't yet fully managed to rid itself of the toxin he'd been drugged with. But as she jogged alongside him, they began to match pace until their footsteps fell in perfect unison, just as their breaths had back in the car.

The camp was dark and silent as they drew near. The power still hadn't been restored. The lodge looked empty, but a light shone from the window of Scott and Gloria's cabin. She guessed they had a battery-powered lamp. Their own cabin was dark, and the shutters were closed. But as they drew close they could hear the faint sound of Matty fussing somewhere within. Wordlessly, Violet reached for Justin's hand. He took it and squeezed it tight for a long moment, before letting go again. Justin knocked softly on the door.

"Emelia? It's Josh and Viv. We know you're in there. Can you open the door? We want to help."

There was no answer. But she could hear Emelia walking across the floor. Violet looked down at the security feed and prayed.

Lord, help us get through to her and resolve this in a way that keeps everybody safe.

Justin leaned toward Violet.

"The lock is pretty flimsy. She didn't know about my backup lock. And that old couch isn't going to put up much resistance either. What I'm worried about is hurting her."

"Emelia," Violet said firmly. "You're here for our help, right? You want Matty safe and taken care of. We can help. We need you to move the couch away from the door, open up and let us come in and help you."

She checked the screen again, but Emelia was shaking so hard she doubted she could pull the couch back if she wanted to.

"Is she clear of the door?" Justin asked.

Violet nodded. "Yeah, you're good."

Justin turned the door handle and threw his full weight against the door, popping the flimsy lock and knocking the couch back a good couple of feet. The cabin floor was littered with Justin and Violet's belongings. Emelia screamed. She dashed across the cabin toward Matty. Violet looked past her to the small child. He was whimpering.

Lord, please let me save him.

"Hey, it's okay." Justin raised his hands, palms up and started across the floor toward her. Violet closed the door to keep out the wind and snow. "We're not going to hurt you. We know you're in trouble, and we just want to help."

"I know who you are!" Emelia shrieked. "I saw the diapers and the baby clothes! You're with them! You killed Frank, didn't you? You're here for Matty! I'm not going to let you take him!"

"We didn't kill Frank," Violet said. "Are you sure he's dead?"

"I think so," Emelia said. "I don't know."

Her words slurred together, and there was an odd, almost singsong tone to her voice. They'd heard that she wasn't well even before they'd taken this case, and over the past twenty-four hours a more complete picture had come into focus. Emelia was frail, her stomach was frequently upset, and it was possible she had hallucinations. But now they could see whatever was ailing her went far beyond that. Her eyes were vacant and glassy. Her skin was so pale it was almost gray.

Then Violet looked past Emelia at Matty. Tears filled his baby blue eyes. Something deep inside Violet's heart ached to scoop him up into her arms, cradle him against her chest and promise to shelter and protect the tiny baby with her life.

"Matty's upset," Justin said. "Why don't you let one of us hold him? You let me hold him before, and it was okay, remember? I promise I'll keep him safe again."

Emelia didn't answer. Instead, she turned and bent down. At first Violet thought she was picking up Matty. But then, it seemed she was rummaging around for something beneath the mattress.

"I'm not even sure she can hear us." Violet's voice dropped. "It's like she's zoned out."

"I think she's been drugged or poisoned," Justin whispered. "Maybe for months. But I just don't know what would cause her symptoms."

Violet took a step back behind Justin, pulled out her phone and texted Anthony.

We need a medical evacuation. Emelia's been poisoned or drugged. Maybe small doses for months.

Look for something that causes: weakness, upset stomach, disorientation and hallucinations.

There was a pause. Then Anthony texted back.

Tessa says rat poison.

Violet's eyes locked on the rattrap in the corner of the room. It was the one poison that had been all over the camp. Ariel had told her that Frank had bought Emelia a special hot chocolate to help her sleep and had recently given her some, too, for Christmas.

Also causes brain swelling. Anthony texted again. Alerting Ariel's hospital now.

Violet texted back. It's possible Frank's been poisoning her hot chocolate.

But why would Frank kill his wife and her best friend? Why do it slowly over time?

Justin's eyes glanced at the text messages on her screen. He sighed sadly.

"You're sick, Emelia," Justin said. "So is Ariel. We think you're sick with the same thing, and it's not your fault. Somebody did this to you, and I'm so sorry they did. We're going to get the paramedics to come and take you to the hospital."

"No!" Emelia spun back.

She raised both hands toward him. She was holding a gun. Violet held her palms up.

"Emelia, put the gun down." Justin's voice was calm and firm.

He took another step toward her, flanking her on the left. Slowly, Violet moved around her on the right.

"You're lying to me. It's just a trick to try and take my baby. I did everything it said in the email! I followed all the rules. You can't take Matty from me."

Did Emelia think they worked for Little Blossoms? Or somebody else who wanted to take the baby?

"Is that how you heard about Little Blossoms?" Violet asked. "Was it a random email? Did someone spam your email with the offer to buy a child?"

Emelia spun toward her. "I can't tell anyone about that!"

A picture was beginning to form in Violet's mind. But it was disjointed, and too many pieces were still missing.

"You got really sick last spring, didn't you?" Violet went on, drawing Emelia's attention toward her so that Justin could get around behind her. "You thought you were pregnant, but you weren't. Then you got an email from Little Blossoms, an advertisement maybe that you found in your spam folder, that promised to solve your problems and make your dreams come true."

Emelia nodded. It was an involuntary gesture, but Violet was certain she was right. Why would someone email a random woman with the news she could buy a baby on the black market? She took another step. The barrel of Emelia's gun followed her.

"How did you convince Frank to pay for the baby?" Violet asked.

"Frank didn't know!" Emelia's voice rose. "He can't know! I used an old account he didn't remember we had! Just like the email said!"

Violet glanced past her to Justin. He was only a few feet away from Emelia now. Matty's cries grew louder. Violet's heart ached. She couldn't imagine how Justin was feeling.

"And Frank is missing now, right?" Violet asked.

"I don't know! I think…they killed him like they killed Ariel!"

"Ariel's not dead" Violet said. "She's in hospital, and we can take you to see her. Please just put the gun down and let me pick up Matty. Then we can all sit down and talk, and it'll be okay."

"No!" Emelia cried. "You're just going to try to take Matty! You can't have him! They sold him to me because I'm a good mother!"

Violet looked at Justin. His eyes widened.

Suddenly Emelia's face paled, as if she just realized what she'd done. "No, no, I didn't mean that. He's my baby."

"Hey." Violet took another step toward Emelia. "It's okay."

"He's mine!" Emelia shouted.

She set Violet in her sights and fired.

The bullet flew wide. Justin threw himself at Emelia, grabbed her by the shoulders and forced her to the ground. She crumpled like wet tissue paper. The gun flew from her hands and skidded across the cabin. Violet rushed past Justin and scooped Matty up into her arms. Justin ran for the weapon. He snatched it up and turned back, expecting to see Emelia lying on the floor where he'd left her.

Instead, she scrambled to her feet and ran out into the snow.

He disarmed her gun and started after her.

"Wait! Don't go!" Violet shouted. He turned. Violet was standing in the back of the cabin, rocking Matty back and forth and shushing him gently. "I don't want to split up. I think we should stick together. She's more danger to herself than she is to anyone else right now, and she won't get far. My worry right now is for this little guy. He's our top priority." She corrected herself. "Our *only* priority."

She wasn't wrong. They had Matty back, but it was far from over yet. They still needed to get him to safety, irrefutably prove his identity and get the warrant needed to keep anyone from taking him away ever again. Something lurched in his chest as he watched the way Violet tenderly cuddled his nephew in his arms and Matty's cries settled.

"What matters most is getting him out of here safely," she said. "And to do that I need backup. You were violently attacked by a masked stranger. If someone comes after me while I'm holding him, I'll have no way to protect him."

"You're right."

The thought of anyone hurting Violet the way he'd been attacked sent something hot and protective surging through his veins. Then he looked down at the tiny baby in her arms. The idea that something could happen to Violet when she was alone with his nephew was almost unthinkable.

"We need backup," she said. "We need someone to

look for Emelia and make sure she's okay. I'm worried she's going to pass out and freeze to death."

"Yeah, me, too," Justin agreed. "We also need to get everyone who remains at this camp to one centralized location for evacuation. There are still several innocent civilians up here, and we don't want anyone getting hurt."

"Me neither," Violet said. "Problem is I don't want to put this little guy at any unnecessary risk."

She leaned down and nuzzled her face against the top of Matty's head. Her eyes misted. Then she looked up again and glanced toward the window. Through the crack in the shutters, he could see the light shining in Scott and Gloria's cabin.

"Both Gloria and Scott were cleared by Anthony and Tessa's background checks," Violet said. "They're good people and I like them, despite your misunderstanding with Scott yesterday. Gloria used to be a trauma nurse, and as a Canadian army ranger, Scott's trained in both emergency first aid and search and rescue. I think you should run over there and brief them. She can get everybody gathered in the lodge, he can go look for Emelia, and they'll be able to explain to the emergency evacuation personnel when they get here."

Justin's jaw clenched. He didn't like the idea of calling in civilians on an active police case. But he hated the idea of leaving Violet alone with Matty at the mercy of whoever might come after them even more.

"Do we have any other options?".

"Not good ones. At least with this plan you're only running next door for a moment. This cabin will still be in sight, and you'll be able to hear me shout if anything happens."

True. He glanced from the determination in her eyes to the tiny child nestled in her arms. The clock was ticking. They didn't have time to argue. His brain knew it was the right call to make. But something inside him balked, and he wasn't sure why. The urge to argue he could somehow do it all on his own and didn't need backup welled up inside him. Instead, he closed his eyes for a moment and prayed to God that her plan would work, and she'd be safe while he was gone.

"I'll be back in a second. Bolt the door behind me with the second lock."

"Will do. And if anything happens while you're out there, just holler."

"You, too."

Justin pulled his jacket hood over his head, slipped outside and waited to hear her lock the door behind him. Then he started across the snow toward Scott and Gloria's cabin. He hadn't noticed the sun setting behind the gray, wintry sky, but now the gloom of January darkness surrounded him. The lights were on, but all was silent as he approached. He knocked on the door.

"Hello?" Gloria's voice came from somewhere inside the cabin.

"Hey, it's Josh! I need to talk to you and your son about something!"

"Come on in!" Gloria called back. "It's not locked."

He turned the knob, pushed the door open and stepped inside the cabin. The living room was empty. Then he felt the butt of a handgun pressed up against the side of his head, heard the door slam shut behind him and realized he'd just walked into a trap.

"Now, here's what's going to happen." Scott's voice was clear and calm. His steady grip on the weapon didn't falter. "You're going to place your hands on your head, nice and slow. You're going to kneel down on the ground. And you're going to tell me exactly who you are and what's really going on here, because I know you're not Josh Cooper of Dukes Wilderness Adventures."

TWELVE

Justin raised his hands above his head, palms up. But he wasn't about to kneel. He sure hoped the others were right about Scott.

"My name is Officer Justin Leacock of the RCMP Major Crimes Unit." He focused on keeping his voice clear and level, despite the obvious threat of the weapon pressed against his temple.

"Which division?" Scott asked.

Right, so just telling him that he was a cop wasn't going to be enough. Justin watched as Gloria appeared in the doorway to the bedroom, close enough that she could listen to the conversation but far enough that she was out of harm's way in case anything happened. Smart. Justin wondered just how long they'd been suspicious of him. He considered trying to bluff.

"I'm with the National Cybercrime Unit"

"The cyber unit?" Scott snorted. "At a wilderness camp with no power? You'll have to do better than that."

Instinctively, Justin turned his head to glare at him when the pressure of the muzzle against his temple made him stop.

"Well, it's the truth." Justin forced a chuckle, hoping that if he pretended he wasn't frustrated and kept things light it would disarm Scott. "I work within the same law enforcement unit that steps in to help when people's grandmothers get scammed into giving strangers their bank details. I'm really good at it, actually."

Just yesterday he'd admitted to Violet that he'd been embarrassed that he hadn't been able to cut it in something grittier when Zablocie had tried to recruit him for the Special Victims Unit. But the truth was, he was really good at the kind of strategizing cybercrimes required.

"Right now, I'm here undercover working on a kidnapping case," Justin added. "I can't give you the full details, but my wife is a corporal with the Missing Persons Unit." There, a little bit of fact and a little bit of keeping up the fiction. No need to let these people know everything. "Now, I have no idea what I've done to get your back up, but I came here to brief you on the situation and ask for your help. I've never exactly been a fan of doing things with a gun to my head. We're on the same side, and we really don't have time for this. So how about you put that weapon away and we can all sit down and talk."

Scott pulled back enough that the gun was no longer pointed directly at Justin and instead sat more casually by his side. Yet his stance and bearing left Justin with no doubt that Scott wouldn't hesitate to draw and fire if he needed to, and that his bullet would not miss.

"And what side would that be?" Scott asked. "You've given me no good reason to trust you now any more than I trusted your first story. You've come across as dodgy and like you're hiding something ever since that first night. After the incident with that one woman and then the bizarre cliffside accident today where a second nearly died, plus the off way you reacted to that search and rescue volunteer, I looked into you."

"And?"

"And a buddy of mine who'd served alongside Sergeant Jeff Cooper confirmed he didn't have a cousin."

Justin debated inviting him back to the cabin to see his badge. But if he did so, they'd see Violet had Matty and that would open up a whole other line of questions that he wasn't in a hurry to answer.

"Look, I don't exactly like briefing two strangers about an ongoing police investigation, but we're outmanned at the moment, and we need your help. There's a rescue helicopter on its way to do a medical evacuation. Unfortunately, Emelia's had another episode and taken off running. We have reason to believe that she's been poisoned and also that there's an unknown threat stalking the camp, who attacked Ariel." *And me.* "We need you to get everyone to the lodge and make sure they stick together until the evacuation arrives and also for you to find Emelia and get her to the lodge if you can. Her husband, Frank, may also be missing."

Or dead.

"Where's her baby now?" Gloria stepped into the room.

"Safe and well," Justin said.

"Safe and well, where?" Scott asked, "And what kind of kidnapping case?"

"I'm afraid I can't divulge that."

"Can't or won't?"

"Won't." Justin had to regain control of the situation, and that included limiting what he let this man know. He wasn't about to trust him with the fact Matty was his own nephew or tell him where Matty was now.

"And why should we trust you with any of this?" Scott pressed.

"Well, we had you vetted," Justin said. "Both of you. Gloria, I know you used to work as an inner-city trauma nurse. Scott, I even know that you dropped out of medical school and loaned your friend tuition money when his wife was murdered by a stalker."

Gloria's eyes widened, and Justin remembered that Anthony had told them that even she might not know that her son had done that. Justin risked lowering his hands to shoulder height to ease the strain on his muscles, but still he kept his hands palm up in a show of good faith that he wasn't about to try anything.

"I get that a tragedy like that can make it really hard to trust people," Justin said, "but you did an incredible thing for your friend, and I know you're good people."

"I didn't ask why you trusted me," Scott said, almost sadly. "I asked why I should trust you?"

What do you want me to tell you? Justin thought. *That my sister suffers from addiction and dropped off the map? That my partner Violet really is my former fiancée whom I foolishly dumped days before my wedding?*

Frustration was building at the back of Justin's neck. What Scott had said back at Ross's sales pitch dinner flickered in the back of his mind. Scott had said he found it hard to build trust with someone who wasn't willing to be honest and vulnerable and who hid their flaws. Well, maybe Justin wasn't exactly in the habit of admitting his problems to anyone. Maybe the guy standing in the middle of the hurricane had to hide his flaws to keep people safe.

"I honestly don't know what to tell you."

Justin heard the sound of a woman screaming outside, only for the sound to be swallowed up by a deafening bang that seemed to linger in the air.

Violet! Justin felt the color drain from his face. Scott could go ahead and shoot him. Justin wasn't going to stand around trying to prove himself when Violet could be in danger. He turned, pushed back through the door and ran toward the noise. A second later he heard both Scott and Gloria running after him. He caught the glimpse of an indistinct figure disappearing through the trees.

Then he saw Emelia. She was lying crumpled in the snow with fresh blood seeping from a gunshot wound to her core.

Please, Lord, in Your mercy, despite what she's done, I beseech You to let her live.

As he reached her side, he heard Gloria's voice. "Step back and let me see her!"

He did so. Gloria rushed past him, yanked off her own scarf, knelt down beside the unconscious woman and pressed it over the bleeding. Scott stood by Justin's side.

Gloria looked up at them. "Who shot her and why?"

"I honestly don't know," Justin said. "But she's a suspect in our investigation, and we think somebody else involved with the crime is trying to silence her. Same for Ariel." He glanced at Scott in the darkness. "If I knew for sure who we could and couldn't trust I'd tell you."

"She shouldn't have passed out from blood loss this quickly," Gloria frowned. "You said she's been poisoned?"

"We think so," Justin said. "Emelia has been sick, erratic and disoriented. Ariel's had unexplained swelling in her brain. We've asked the hospital to run full toxicology scans on them both."

Gloria shared a long, silent look with her son. Then she looked down at her patient.

"We need to keep pressure on the wound or she's going to lose a lot of blood. I don't want to move her, but we can't leave her out here. You said search and rescue are on their way?"

"They are."

"Can we safely transport her to the lodge?" Scott turned to Gloria.

"We can," she said, "if you can carry her while I keep pressure on her wound."

Justin watched as Scott closed his eyes, took a deep breath and let it out slowly. When he opened his eyes again, there was fresh resolve in his gaze like a decision had been made.

"We'll take Emelia to the lodge," Scott said, "ring the triangle, summon people to join us and tell them evacuation is coming. We'll keep everyone together, and while my mother tends to Gloria, I'll be able to protect everyone until rescue arrives. Now, is there anything else you're not telling me that I need to know?"

"Emelia is a suspect in a pretty serious case," Justin said. "Someone may want to silence her, so don't let anyone, including her husband, get too close to her until authorities arrive."

"Understood," Scott said. "Contact the paramedics and let them know there's a gunshot victim."

"Will do." Justin watched as Gloria carefully packed snow on Emelia's wound, then placed her scarf back over it again. Scott bent down and gently picked Emelia up, while his mother hovered at her side.

"Thank you," Justin said.

He looked again at Emelia, the woman who'd paid kidnappers to steal his newborn nephew from the hospital. She looked so weak and fragile in the army ranger's arms. Worries cascaded through Justin's mind. What if Emelia woke up and told him a whole different story? What if they didn't make it to the lodge safely? Or someone attacked the lodge?

What if something went wrong?

Then his gaze drifted back to the cabin where he'd left Violet and Matty. For all the things he didn't know, there was one thing he knew for certain—there was a gunman in the woods who wouldn't hesitate to shoot whoever he considered a target.

Fear bubbled up inside him—one that Justin hadn't felt this strongly since the day he'd made the terrible decision to tell the woman he loved that he wouldn't be her husband.

He couldn't do it all. He couldn't be in two places at once. What if he dropped the ball and something terrible happened?

Scott and Gloria were already making their way

across the snow to the lodge. Justin turned and ran back to the cabin where he'd left Violet. The snow was beginning to fall again, fast and thick, obscuring his vision. He reached the cabin, knocked and called out. "Hey, Viv, it's me."

She unlocked the door and ushered him inside. Justin locked and bolted the door behind him. He noticed that she'd gathered up all of Matty's baby gear and set it on the couch. The snowsuit and chest harness lay on the coffee table. She'd also heated a small pot of water on top of the wood-burning stove, which Justin assumed was to make formula.

Matty sat contentedly in the crook of Violet's arm, wearing a fresh set of clean clothes and drinking from a baby bottle. The baby's blue eyes gazed at his uncle.

Here you are. Healthy, safe and loved.

The triangle sounded in the distance, summoning everyone to the lodge.

"Are you okay?" Violet searched his face. "I heard gunfire."

"Emelia's been shot," he said. "I need to call Anthony."

She shifted Matty in her arms, took out her phone and handed it to him. Then she quickly steadied the bottle again for Matty.

Justin dialed Anthony.

"Hello," Anthony answered. "No word from the hospital yet—"

"Emelia's been shot," Justin said. "She's still alive, but I'm not sure she's stable. Scott and Gloria are with her now, and they've taken her to the lodge."

"Did you see who—"

His voice cut off.

"Hello? Hello? Can you hear me?"

The call had dropped. Justin dialed again. This time he couldn't get through.

He turned to Violet. "I've lost them."

"Keep trying."

He hit Redial. The call failed again.

"Did you see who shot Emelia?" Violet asked.

Justin shook his head. Matty drained the bottle. Violet shifted Matty into Justin's left arm, poured the hot water into a thermos and started packing Matty's gear back in the backpack.

"Everything go okay with Scott and Gloria?" Violet asked.

"Scott held me at gunpoint and told me he knew I wasn't who I said I was." Justin tried the call again. It didn't even ring. "Apparently, I'm not as good at undercover work as I'd like to think I am."

"Or Scott is just overly suspicious after what happened to his friend's wife," Violet interjected.

"Either way he doesn't trust me. But I'm confident he and his mom will do their very best to keep Emelia alive and well and get everyone to the lodge for evacuation."

Their doorknob rattled. It seemed someone was trying to let themselves into their cabin, and they hadn't bothered to knock first.

"Who's that?" Violet mouthed silently.

Justin shook his head and mouthed back, "I don't know."

A key turned in the lock. Whoever was there had a

staff master key. Justin was thankful he'd remembered to do the bolt as well.

"Hey, just give us a second!" Violet called out loudly and cheerfully, as if she knew exactly who was on the other side of the door and had been expecting them.

No answer.

Justin handed her the baby, then he snatched the harness up off the couch, put his arms through the straps and quickly snapped it on over his chest. She slid Matty into his snowsuit.

The doorknob turned, and the door began to creak open.

They didn't wait to see who was on the other side.

Violet ran into the bedroom with Matty. Justin grabbed the bag of baby gear and entered the other room just one step behind her. He slammed the bedroom door and fastened the lock. Violet did up the zipper on Matty's snowsuit. The cabin's front door slammed against the backup lock Justin had brought. Then it crashed again and again, as if whoever was on the other side was trying to break it down.

Matty whimpered. Wordlessly, Justin took the tiny child from Violet's arms and brushed a kiss over his head.

Lord, please help me protect him and keep him safe.

The sound of gunfire shook the cabin around them. Seemed their intruder had given up on kicking and had decided to shoot the door right off the hinges. They heard wood splinter and heavy boots stepping over the threshold and onto the living room floor.

"We've got to get out of here," Violet said.

The fierce determination and trust that filled her gaze took his breath away.

He slid Matty into the chest harness. She ran for the window, threw the shutters open, braced both hands against the thin, single-glass pane in the window and shoved with all her might. The glass popped out. She climbed through.

Furniture crashed in the living room behind him. Matty opened his mouth and wailed. Justin jumped through the window out into the snow to find Violet crouched by the wall waiting for him. Together they ran for the forest and took shelter behind the trees. Only then did Justin look back.

A man was standing in the window they'd leaped through moments ago. His ski mask was torn at the side just enough that Justin recognized him.

It was Curly, the Little Blossoms operative who'd kidnapped Matty from the hospital and fired at Violet when she'd grabbed the DNA samples from the DuBois cottage. He hopped out through the window.

They turned and ran into the forest as Curly opened fire.

Violet and Justin ran through the woods, pressing deeper and deeper through the thick trees. Tactical questions and scenarios shot rapid-fire through her mind. Rescuing the life of the precious child now strapped to Justin's chest was all that mattered. She couldn't stop to engage with the enemy pursuing them without risking the baby's life. Unless she and Justin split up, which couldn't happen because it would just leave whoever was holding the baby in greater danger.

They had to stick together and evade Curly.

The evening sky drew darker around her. Her eyes struggled to adjust to the dying light. A bullet sounded from behind them and struck a tree to their right. The bark exploded like shrapnel.

Suddenly, all of her usual concerns paled in comparison to the magnitude of the responsibility she and Justin were now carrying.

It's not just my life that's on the line anymore, Lord. Protecting Matty is all that matters.

"We need a plan to get out of this camp!" she called. "I don't think hiding's going to work."

"Agreed. Just trying to get my bearings and figure out where we are." His breaths were coming hard and fast. "If I remember our tour of the grounds correctly, we should be hitting a path with green markers any moment now." That was the circular path that led all the way around the camp and branched off into other paths that led to the cliffs with the broken ski lift and the climbing hut where Ariel had fallen. "We just have to figure out how to get from there to the hiking paths Lorenzo told us about. Ross said there was a snowmobile in the shed at the bottom of the tobogganing hill."

Another burst of gunfire shook the trees. Seemed like Curly had reloaded and was now just shooting blindly in their direction. Suddenly the trees parted in front of them.

"Get ready to jump!" Justin shouted.

The path was a good five feet below them. Violet

leaped, with Justin alongside her, and nearly fell to her knees before she managed to regain her balance.

"Which way do we go?" she called.

"Right!"

They ran down the green path. Their feet sprinted faster now that they were on level ground. But once Curly caught them in his sights, he'd have a clear shot of them.

"We need to find cover!" she said.

The broken ski lift dangled in the air ahead of them. Then she saw the mounds of toboggans covered in tarps.

"How do you feel about taking a shortcut down the mountain?"

"Like it's a ridiculous idea," Violet called back. "But the best one we've got."

Anything to put as much distance as possible between them and the man pursuing them. They reached the first pile of toboggans and ducked low behind it. Justin lifted the tarp and pulled one out. It was the shape and size of an inflatable lifeboat, with reinforced rubber sides.

Justin whispered a prayer of thanksgiving.

"Are you confident you'll be able to keep Matty safe?" she asked.

"I am. You sit in the front and steer. I'll push us off and use my feet to brake and slow us down."

She climbed in and grabbed hold of a piece of yellow rope that acted as the steering wheel. Snow pelted down around them in the darkness. She could barely see ten feet in front of her. Then she felt the toboggan lurch forward and Justin's weight land in the sled behind her. His left arm wrapped around her waist. His head leaned against her shoulder as he sheltered Matty with his body.

They slid down the mountain away from the camp. White snowflakes filled her view, flying toward her against the gray haze like a myriad of stars. Freezing wind brushed past her cheeks and nipped at her skin.

A fresh flurry of bullets shook the air behind them. She wondered if Curly had even realized where they'd gone or if from his perspective they'd just suddenly disappeared. She held tightly onto the rope and focused on the path ahead, calling out directions for Justin to lean to one side or the other, and drag his foot to slow them down, as rocks and trees materialized in the gloom.

The ground leveled out beneath them, and they skidded to a stop. Silence fell, punctuated only by the sounds of their own ragged breath and the distant roar of a rescue helicopter heading for the lodge.

Justin gasped. "All good?"

"All good. You?"

"Yeah, we're are all good."

Something soft choked in Justin's throat. She looked back. His head was bent low over the tiny baby still nestled safely against him. His hand cupped Matty's cheek gently, and the baby looked so tiny in his uncle's protective palm.

I promise, I'll do everything in my power to make sure Matty is safe and home with you, where he belongs.

They climbed out of the toboggan, searched the area and found a first aid shed a couple of yards away. The door was unlocked. They stepped inside and shone their flashlights around. It was larger than she'd expected, with both a table and first aid cot and a snowmobile under the tarp. Justin handed Matty to Violet, and then he tried to start the snowmobile. The engine didn't start. He checked the gas tank.

"It's empty. Guess that means we're walking."

All the way back down the mountain? How long would that take them? At least an hour, and they'd be vulnerable the whole time to both the elements and whoever might be hunting them. She checked her phone. The signal was dead. She tried to call Anthony anyway, but of course the call didn't go through.

Unexpectedly and without warning, the worry and fear she'd been managing to keep at bay suddenly caught up with her, catching her off guard and flooding her heart. Tears of frustration filled her eyes and, to her embarrassment, began to slide down her cheeks.

"Hey," Justin said, softly. "It's okay."

"No. It's not, and it hasn't been for a long time. We are in the middle of the woods, in the snow, with a baby we took from the incredibly ill woman who had bought him from criminals, one of whom just tried to kill us. And we still haven't even proved he's your nephew."

She shifted Matty up higher onto her shoulder. She could feel his warmth against her heart.

"It's my job to protect these babies and stop the Little Blossoms Syndicate," she went on. "I've been throwing myself into this case seven days a week, and they're still out there. Every time we've gotten a glimmer of hope, something else has happened. I started to build a connection with Ariel, and now she's in hospital fighting for her life. Maybe because of me. I got the DNA sample we needed, and the mountain caved in. And now, we're stuck here having to walk down the mountain, not even knowing if the paths we're going to take are even still intact."

Hot tears were falling faster now than she could wipe them away. As if they'd been building up for months and she couldn't hold them back any longer.

"Everybody blamed you when our engagement fell apart," she said. "Everyone told me that there was nothing wrong with me and everything the matter with you. But who's to say that if you had come to me last spring and honestly told me everything you were struggling with that I could have helped? What if you were right to underestimate me?"

"Hey, I never underestimated you." Justin stepped forward, cradled her face in his hand and wiped the tears away with his thumb. "You are the strongest woman I've met. If I'd been brave enough to come to you with my problems and trust you with what I was going through, maybe you couldn't have solved anything, but I know my life would've been immeasurably better for having you in it."

For a long moment, his eyes looked deeply into hers. Then he looked down at the small child sitting in her arms in between them.

"We're safe and we're together." Justin's voice grew husky. "Despite everything we've gone through, we've made it this far. I haven't lost you, you haven't lost me, and we've got the most important person in this whole operation away from the criminals. I'm sorry for thinking there was anything that mattered more than this."

His fingertips lightly brushed against her hair. "I have unlimited and unwavering faith in you. And yeah, it'll be cold and hard, not to mention tiring, but we're going to make it down this mountain, together, one step at a time."

She leaned forward and rested her forehead against his for a long moment.

"Thank you. I needed that."

He wrapped his arms around her and Matty and held them both tight. For a long moment she let herself rest in his strength. Then she straightened up, and he pulled away.

Justin moved the chest harness inside his coat for extra warmth. Violet made up a fresh bottle with one hand while she bounced Matty in the other. Then after Matty had eaten a little more, Justin strapped the baby to his chest again and zipped his coat up around them both, making sure Matty's tiny hood was up and he was sheltered from the elements.

They set off into the snow. It was falling thicker now, like small, wet snowballs tumbling from the sky. The lingering gray sky had darkened almost to black. They switched their flashlights on the lowest setting and kept them close to the ground. It didn't take long for them to find the brightly colored paint smudges marking the trees and showing them the way down the mountain.

It was a long, slow journey. They jogged as much as they could, without talking except for tossing small words of encouragement back and forth when one or the other of them started to flag. At times the path was so steep or the snow so deep that they had no choice but to slow to a crawl.

They passed small huts on the paths, where they paused to check on Matty and switch who was carrying him on their chest.

Her limbs ached with exhaustion. Her exposed skin stung from the cold. Her lungs burned with each breath. But they trudged on, footstep by footstep, down the side of the mountain. Every now and then she'd catch Justin's eye, see his smile, feel a fresh surge of oxygen fill her veins and know without even the smallest shadow of a doubt that there was nobody else she'd rather be going through this ordeal with.

She'd thought she'd loved this strong, funny, brave, incredible, caring man back on the day she'd agreed to marry him. But whatever she'd felt then was nothing compared to what beat through her heart now.

How would she ever go back to her normal life away from him after this?

They'd been plodding through the woods for over an hour when she heard the crunch of footsteps in the darkness. They ducked behind a tree. Her hands rose to protect Matty, who was now strapped to her chest.

Justin stepped in front of her and reached for his weapon.

"Stay behind me," he whispered. "If whoever's out here thinks they're going to lay a hand on either of you, they're going to have to go through me first."

THIRTEEN

"Violet!" Her brother's voice cut through the wintry air. "Justin! Shout if you can hear me!"

"Anthony!" Joy and relief cascaded through her heart. "We're here!"

Justin sheathed his weapon. They ran toward the sound of Anthony and Tessa calling their names. Moments later she saw her tall, sensible brother charging toward them. He was trailed by his wife, whose thick brown curls were covered in snow.

Anthony and Tessa wrapped their arms around Violet. Then Violet reached out for Justin, and he joined in their group hug, with Matty enveloped in the middle of the scrum.

"How did you find us?" Violet asked.

"GPS," Anthony said. "Remember? We parked on the side of the road, as close as we could to your signal, and made our way up on foot."

The huddle broke, and she watched as Anthony looked down at the tiny bundle in her arms. Something softened in her big brother's eyes.

"I take it this little guy is our kidnapped baby?"

"Anthony, Tessa," Justin said. "Meet my nephew. Safe, well and free from the people who kidnapped him."

"Thank You, God," Anthony breathed out the prayer, and the others whispered an amen.

"Now what we've got to do is get his DNA to a lab to prove what we already know," Violet said, "and make sure the DuBois can never get their hands on him again."

"We've got a friend in the unit waiting back at the safe house to take it straight to the lab," Anthony said. "It might take a few hours, but we should have the results by morning."

They jogged through the woods back to Anthony's truck, saving any more debriefing and conversation until they were inside, warm and on the move.

They reached Anthony's double-cabbed truck to find that he'd installed a newborn car seat in the back for Matty. They all piled in, with Anthony driving, Tessa in the passenger seat and Justin and Violet in the back with Matty.

The baby's eyes widened as the truck began to roll, as if he wondered where he was going, and Violet silently promised him that he would be safe.

"Good news first," Anthony said, as he drove down the snow-covered roads. "We were right about the rat poison. Doctors found rodenticide in Ariel's system. The levels were low enough they were able to start treatment, and her condition is improving."

"That's great," Violet said.

"Also, the evacuation went well. All the remaining camp staff, the owner, Ross, Gloria, Scott and Emelia were all evacuated safely."

"Not Frank?" Justin asked.

"No. They did a quick perimeter search and even sent a runner to his cottage. But they couldn't find him."

Violet met Justin's gaze across the back seat.

"Then where is he?" she asked. "Is he even still alive?"

"They have no idea," Anthony said. "Emelia hasn't regained consciousness yet, and depending on how she was poisoned and the amount of rodenticide in her system, she might need medical care for the rest of her life."

Justin blew out a hard breath. "This whole situation is so incredibly sad. Especially if it turns out we're right and her own husband has been poisoning her."

"But again, why would he do that?" Violet wondered aloud.

"I may have an answer to that," Tessa said. "While my husband was researching official channels, I reached out to my private detective sources online. I have a friend in Norway who's a private detective, and she was able to do some digging with contacts she had."

"And?" Justin asked.

"Oh, it's all gossip, but it's a doozy." Tessa turned around and looked at them between the seats. "Frank made several trips to visit his grandmother this year to ask for money. He also asked for permission to divorce his wife. Apparently, Grandma holds the purse strings pretty tightly, and she's cut a lot of people off for what she considers irresponsible living."

"And judging by what I dug up at the start of all this about Frank cheating on his wife," Justin said, "Granny probably considers him incredibly irresponsible."

"Yup," Tessa said. "He dropped out of two universities without completing his degree, blew through his trust fund, has a failed athletic career and has done a lot of philandering. She is not a fan of her youngest grandson. In fact, a few months ago Frank's grandmother announced that she'd decided to split her considerable wealth equally between her six great grandchildren. Each great-grandchild would get a trust worth approximately ten million dollars."

Justin whistled.

"So, if Frank divorced his wife and didn't produce a child, he'd inherit nothing," Justin said. "But if he and Emelia had a child, Matty would get a ten-million-dollar trust, which Frank could find ways to siphon off. Even if his wife then passed away."

"Yuppers," Tessa said. "Motive to kill his wife and buy a child."

"In which case maybe the reason he put it all on Emelia's shoulders, kept his hands clean and wasn't even in the country when Matty was snatched and sold to her was to cover his tracks if he was caught," Justin said. "If I could get access to Emelia's emails, I might be able to prove whether Frank had anything to do with the original email about Little Blossoms."

It all made sense, Violet thought. Had they finally solved the mystery? Frank wanted to be rid of his wife, but he needed to make it look like she died of natural causes, so he poisoned her. He needed a baby to keep the family money flowing, so he manipulated Emelia into buying one. She couldn't do it alone, so she manipulated kindhearted and naive Ariel into helping her with some story about rescuing a baby in need. Then

Little Blossoms sent Curly to make sure the DuBois family kept the origin of baby Matty secret, and when Ariel and Emelia seemed to threaten that secret, Curly tried to kill them.

And yet, a misgiving niggled at the back of her mind. There was still something they were missing, but she couldn't figure out what. She'd been running on adrenaline for hours. Her body ached, and her brain cried out for sleep.

We're so close to solving this, Lord. Help me figure out what I'm missing and close this case for good.

The safe house was a low, white-paneled bungalow set down a long and winding forest road. Anthony parked in front of the house, Justin unbuckled Matty's car seat and they all walked inside.

An unmarked police vehicle was sitting in the driveway. Violet handed the officer behind the wheel Matty's bottles and blanket in the evidence bag, and he sped off.

A sigh of relief rolled off Violet's shoulders. It would take at least two hours for the samples to get to the lab and then a few hours for the tests. But by morning they'd have the proof they needed.

Anthony and Tessa walked into the kitchen, saying something about food. Justin set Matty down on the floor in the car seat, sat beside him and unzipped his snowsuit. Violet dropped onto the couch, feeling like a marionette whose strings had just been cut.

Her phone started to ping. It had managed to connect to the house's Wi-Fi signal, and a flood of missed messages were coming in. She glanced at the screen and felt the blood drain from her face.

"I've missed seven calls from Zablocie. He's left me multiple texts telling me to call him and also a voice mail."

She pressed the voice mail button and put it on speakerphone. Her boss's voice filled the room.

"I need you to call me as soon as you get this," Her usually unflappable boss sounded downright worried. "Don't talk to law enforcement. Don't trust anyone. Do nothing until you talk to me. Otherwise, I won't be able to protect you."

Violet looked at Justin. "Protect me? Protect me from what?"

Anthony rushed in from the kitchen clutching his phone, with Tessa on his heels. Her brother's face was ashen.

"I've just heard that Zablocie has been suspended for disobeying a direct order from his superior officer."

Justin leaped to his feet. Fear stabbed Violet's heart. What was happening?

The deafening blare of police sirens rushing down the driveway toward the house made Justin leap to his feet. Red and blue lights flashed outside, filling the windows with their glare. She glanced through the curtains to see RCMP Emergency Response Team officers swarming the house in full body armor, as if preparing to take down a criminal hideout.

This had to be what Zablocie had wanted to warn her about, but now it was too late.

"Police! Open up!" Voices boomed. Fists pounded on the door, with the kind of insistent knock that Violet recognized as a mere formality before the door was broken down.

Anthony glanced at the others. His face was grave, and his badge was already in his hand. "I have seniority, and I arranged this RCMP safe house in my name. I don't know what this is, but I'm the one who should open the door."

"Okay," Violet said.

Her brother opened the door with his badge held high and his face set like flint.

"I'm Sergeant Anthony Jones of the RCMP Major Crimes' Unsolved Homicide Unit," he announced like his name was a declaration of non-surrender. "Inside here with me are Corporal Violet Jones with Missing Persons, Officer Justin Leacock of Cybercrimes, my wife, Tessa Jones, and a minor child we rescued as part of an ongoing investigation. How may I help you?"

She counted at least six law enforcement vehicles and over a dozen heavily armed officers. But what worried her most was the chauffeured black car that had pulled in behind them. Chief Superintendent Zablocie's superior officer, Assistant Commissioner Davey, stepped out of the back, followed by Frank DuBois. Zablocie had warned them from the very start that Frank's grandmother had powerful allies high up in the government and law enforcement. He'd also said that one slipup could end their careers.

"Sorry to disturb you, Sergeant," the officer at the door said politely. "But we have reason to believe that a minor child has been kidnapped and is being held on this premises. His father has obtained a court order to have the child removed and returned to his custody immediately."

"Yes, there's a kid on the premises," Justin said. "But that man is not the child's father."

Matty began to cry. Justin turned toward him to settle his tears.

"Sir, I'm going to have to ask you to step back from the child," the lead officer said, "and let his father take him."

"I just told you, he's not his father!" Justin's voice rose.

Gently, Violet picked Matty up from the car seat, cradled him to her chest and hushed his tears, ignoring the officer's order to put him down. They'd have to arrest her first.

Help us Lord. What is happening? What do I do? How do I stop it?

Voices rose around her as the police repeated their instructions, Anthony demanded to see everyone's badges and Justin made it clear that no one was about to get anywhere near Matty. Then she heard the squeal of an old pickup truck rushing down the driveway and slamming on its brakes.

Zablocie leaped out, raised his hands and pushed his way into the fray.

"Give me a moment with my team," he said, "and I'm certain we can resolve this."

Zablocie rushed past them through the front door and shut it behind him.

"What's happening?" Violet asked. "We heard you'd been suspended!"

"They've got it all wrong," Justin said. "This is my nephew! I give you my word."

"I believe you." Zablocie answered Justin first. Then he looked around at the others. "Unfortunately, Frank DuBois's grandmother doesn't and has managed to convince a few people above my pay grade that you made a mistake, misidentified his child, harassed an innocent man and stole his child. I was ordered to tell my superior officer where you'd taken the child, and I refused in no uncertain terms. Things got heated. They told me to step aside so they could figure out who'd been assigned to assist you and which safe house you were using." He sighed. "So, yes, I have been suspended."

Violet sucked in a breath.

"You can't be serious!" Justin said. "How could anyone believe him?"

"He's produced a certified copy of a DNA test proving that he's Matty's biological father." He glanced at Justin. "And a birth certificate declaring him the father, purportedly signed by your sister, Sadie."

Frustration, bordering on panic, welled up inside Justin.

"Surely you realize how ridiculous this is!" Justin said. "He forged that birth certificate, my sister's signature and that DNA evidence. That man is not the father of my sister's child!"

"Do you have any proof at all to back that up?" Zablocie demanded. "Or a way to reach her on the phone? Because last I heard you haven't spoken to her in weeks, and she's provided no assistance to this investigation."

Justin clenched his jaw and shook his head. No, he still didn't know where Sadie was.

"Frank DuBois admits to being habitually unfaithful to his wife with various women he picked up in bars in downtown Vancouver," Zablocie continued. His words came fast and urgent. "He claimed that he met your sister last spring in a rough part of the city and had a brief dalliance with her, which he kept secret from his wife. When Sadie found out she was pregnant, she called him and agreed to give Frank full custody of his son and give up all parental rights so that Emelia could adopt him."

"That's ridiculous," Justin said. "How does he explain Curly stealing the kid from the hospital?"

"All a big, unfortunate misunderstanding that he's very apologetic about," Zablocie said. "Because he was out of the country when his son was born, he sent an associate to pick him up from the hospital. His associate isn't from this part of the world and doesn't speak much English. He didn't even realize that anyone thought Matty had been kidnapped, or he'd have sorted all this sooner."

"But, sir!" Justin's voice rose. "We believe he'd been poisoning his wife!"

"He claims his wife has been poisoning herself in order to get attention and sympathy," Zablocie went on, "and that the whole reason he was moving overseas was to get her the help she needs. I'm sure his lawyer will argue before a judge that nothing Emelia told us about the baby is credible."

Justin's hands clenched into fists. He opened his mouth to argue, but before he could speak he felt Anthony place a brotherly hand on his shoulder.

"You're fighting the wrong person," Anthony said, softly. "Obviously, Zablocie doesn't believe Frank. He's on your side. Otherwise, he wouldn't have gone to bat for you."

And gotten suspended.

"Last thing we want right now is for you to be suspended or, even worse, arrested." Anthony glanced at Violet, who was still holding Matty. "Either of you. So go take a breath, pray and figure out what our next move is. We'll stay here and hold them off as long as we can."

Justin nodded.

"It's okay. I'm okay." Justin realized how hollow he sounded.

Violet slid Matty into Justin's arms. He turned and walked blindly down the hallway, into a nursery with a small crib and change table set up against the wall and then out through a sliding door and onto a wooden deck. There Justin sank to his knees with his nephew in his arms, his own legs seemingly unwilling to carry him any farther.

Justin gazed out into the trees. Snow and darkness filled his eyes. The sounds of the chaos at the front of the house faded until all he could hear was the sound of Matty's little breaths mingling with his.

Help me, Lord. I can't lose him again.

Then he heard the crunch of footsteps in the snow and felt comforting hands brush his shoulder. He turned and looked up at Violet. Her body was illuminated by the soft glow of the house. Snow clung to her hair. Tears streaked her beautiful face. Justin stood, shifted Matty into one arm and wrapped the other around Violet's waist. Her fingers slid up into his hair. He kissed the tears from her cheeks. Then slowly and gently, his lips met hers in a kiss so tender it was like they were each tying to take away the other's fear and pain.

Violet stepped back out of his arms, and her fierce eyes locked on his face.

"We can't let Frank take him," she said. "How do we stop him?"

"I don't know—"

"Yes, you do. You're the guy who can fix any problem."

Or at least, who always tried to.

"Who's Matty's real biological father?" Violet asked.

"Matty's dad was a drug dealer and spree killer named Lee, who killed multiple people, including two police officers," Justin admitted. "He was taken out by a cop before she even found out she was pregnant. I told her she didn't have to put his name on the birth certificate, and I promised I'd never tell anyone. I honestly thought I was protecting her and Matty."

"You need to tell Zablocie that. *All* of that."

"But I can't prove that's what she told me."

"Then, how do we prove it?"

Then it hit him.

"We can't get Frank's DNA without a court order," Justin said. "But Lee's DNA is in the system. We have Matty's DNA tested against Lee's to prove Frank is not his father."

Violet crossed her arms and nodded. "Go on."

"I'd walk through every dark corner of Vancouver where Sadie has been known to hide out," Justin said, "and tell everyone who'll talk to me that Sadie's child is about to be whisked overseas by a man who I believe is a kidnapper, human trafficker and attempted murderer and that she can save Matty by just confirming he's not her son's father. Right now, if people do know where she is, they're not about to tell a cop, even if he's her brother. This appeal might be enough to get her to reach out to me. But we don't have that kind of time."

He ran both hands through his hair.

"Violet, I can't do all this alone."

Even though that much was clear, he felt something new move through his heart as he said the words, as if he was finally ready to believe them.

I can't do it alone, Lord. And I've been trying to for so long. Help me ask for help. And help me get the kind of help I need.

He looked down at the tiny baby in his arms. Matty had fallen asleep. Then Justin stepped toward Violet and took her hand again.

"*We* can't do this alone," he clarified. "We need help."

"Come on, then. Let's go get help."

He ran back into the house and through to the living room, feeling fresh determination and focus fill his core. Zablocie, Anthony and Tessa turned to face them.

"Okay," Justin said. "We have a plan, and to mobilize it, we're going to call in a whole lot of favors."

He briefed them quickly and clearly, outlining exactly who the father of Sadie's child was and what they needed to prove it. Then they set to work. Tessa called every informant she had as a private eye who might be able to hit the streets and ask around about Sadie, while Justin did the same with his colleagues at the RCMP.

Violet contacted the lab, outlined the DNA test they needed and got them to agree to expedite it. Anthony and Zablocie took turns between stalling the officers at the door and calling every senior law enforcement, judicial and political contact they had to plead their case.

Minutes ticked past. Slowly the number of cars and officers in the driveway began to trickle away, as word got around the RCMP of the phone battle being waged, and higher-ups apparently decided to discretely remove their own people from the fray. Zablocie's superior officer left, too. Finally only a handful of officers remained.

"Frank's left!" Violet looked out through the curtains, then back at Justin. "Do you think he's given up?"

"Maybe," Justin said. "I don't think he ever wanted a son. He just wanted a way to get a chunk of his inheritance. And now that he sees which way the wind is blowing, he'll abandon his battle and just flee the country before we can issue a warrant for child trafficking and attempted murder."

Justin shifted Matty from one arm to another. The baby had begun to fuss and was moments away from full-out crying.

"Justin!" Tessa ran across the living room toward him, holding out her phone. "I've got your sister on the phone for you!"

Prayers of thanksgiving filled Justin's heart.

"Do you want me to hold Matty while you take it?"

"Yeah, thanks, Violet." Justin handed the precious bundle to her. "Heads up, I think he needs to be changed."

Violet laughed.

"I'm sure I can handle it. I'll see if he'll go down for

a nap, too. But keep an eye on my phone. We should have the DNA results in less than ten."

She set her phone on the coffee table, picked up the rucksack of baby supplies and walked down the hall-way to the room with the crib in it.

Justin held the phone to his ear.

"Sadie? Are you there?"

"Justin?" His sister's breathless voice came down the phone. "Is that really you?"

"Yeah, sis, it's me."

"There's this lady here. She says she's a friend of a friend of yours or something. She showed me this pic-ture of a man and asked me if I know him and that he's saying he's my kid's dad. But I've never seen him be-fore!" Her voice rose. "I don't know who he is, and I never signed anything. You can't let him take the baby anywhere! He's not his dad!"

"Hey, it's okay," Justin said, softly. "He's not taking your son anywhere. I found your little baby, and he's safe here with me."

His sister sniffed. "Really?"

"I promise. I do need you to help me, by signing some papers about the fact you want him to live with me, and of course his birth certificate. But I won't let anyone hurt him. I promise."

Violet's phone rang. Tessa picked it up.

"And we've got the DNA results!" Tessa called. "Frank DuBois is definitely not the father!"

"Well, it's about time." Zablocie's hands rose. "I feel like I've been tap-dancing my feet off for the past half an hour." He stuck out his hand toward Tessa. "Here, let me see it. I've got some dolts I want to send those results to immediately."

Justin laughed as joy and relief washed through his core. Then he heard the muffled noise of what sounded like a thud hitting the floor, followed by the sudden sound of Matty crying.

"Hang on one second, Sadie. I just need to check on Violet."

He muted the call and started for the nursery. Cold wind whipped through the house.

"Hey, Violet? Everything okay?"

Justin's footsteps quickened. He rushed into the nursery. The room was empty except for Matty who was lying in the crib waving all four limbs in protest.

"Violet? Where are you?"

Surely she wouldn't just abandon Matty alone like this. The door was wide open. Footsteps marred the ground. Then he saw the trail of footprints leading into the trees. A green and unmarked bottle lay in the snow. Carefully, Justin slid on a glove and picked it up. The sickly smell of chloroform filled his senses. Fresh fear tightened in his chest, blocking his ability to breathe.

Violet had been drugged. She'd been kidnapped and now she was gone.

FOURTEEN

The first thing that hit Violet's senses when her foggy brain swam back to consciousness was the low rumble of an engine underneath the floor she was lying on. The second was the sound of Frank's voice angrily shouting at someone. "No cops! If I so much as see a vehicle on the ground or a light in the sky, I'll kill her!"

Nobody answered. Was he yelling into a phone? She jolted upright, thinking for a moment she was somehow back in the safe house's nursery, feeling strong hands grab her from behind and clamp a chloroform-soaked cloth over her face.

"I'm not going to let you take him!" Violet tried to shout. But her words slurred and ran together like gibberish. She struggled to sit up. Only then did she realize her hands were tied behind her back.

"Oh, she's awake," Frank's voice said dryly, somewhere on the edges of her mind. It was a far cry from the shouting he'd been doing just moments ago. "Guess you didn't kill her, after all. I was worried you'd gone overboard and we'd lost our hostage."

Who was he talking to? She heard the sound of ice

clinking inside a glass. The engines rumbled louder. She couldn't hear Matty anywhere. She was their only hostage? Had they left Matty behind?

Lord, help me get my wits about me, figure out where I am and get out of here! Please give Justin and my brother the information they need to rescue me. Please may Matty be all right!

"Go check on her!" Frank added.

"She's fine," an unfamiliar voice said. It was male and heavily accented. "She's not going anywhere."

Violet let her body go limp to buy herself time, by letting them think she'd passed out again. She took a long, deep breath, and slowly the space around her came into focus. Her wrists were tied with what felt like some kind of fabric. But not overly tightly, maybe because she'd been limp and unconscious when they'd bound her. She was lying on a blue patterned rug. Walls curved around her with oval windows looking out into the darkness. Fear shot down her spine. She was on a small airplane. It was a private jet by the look of it, with two pairs of facing seats, one on each side. They'd left her lying on the floor in the back. Frank sat in one seat drinking what looked like alcohol from a thick, square glass. Curly stretched out on a seat across the aisle from him with his hat pulled down over his face and his arms crossed.

How was he planning on leaving the country? The RCMP must've been issued a warrant by now and had officers fanned out across the province looking for him. Then her drug-addled mind caught up with the words she'd heard him shouting on the phone to someone.

She was Frank's ticket out of the country.

"When are we getting out of here?" Frank snapped angrily.

"I don't know!"

"Get in the cockpit and tell them to start the plane, now!" Frank ordered Curly. "Wave a gun at them if you have to!"

Curly dutifully pulled his weapon and entered the cockpit. The engines hummed louder. Violet slid her body over to the closet seat and pivoted so that her back was against what had been Curly's seat. She slipped the fabric tying her hands over the metal edge of the bolts that fastened it to the floor and pulled.

"Hey!" Frank snapped. "What are you doing? Stop wriggling around back there!"

She ignored him, clenched her teeth and pulled harder. The fabric tore. She wriggled her hands free.

"I told you to stop it!" Frank charged at her.

She looked up as he loomed over her, red-faced and furious. Was this how he'd looked to Emelia? Was this how he'd have been with Matty? She struggled to her feet, desperately willing her shaky legs to hold her up long enough that she could fight back and get away.

Frank lunged, grabbed her by the neck and yanked her upright. He pushed her up against the curved wall of the plane, putting just enough pressure to cause her pain without enough to make her pass out. The jet began to taxi down the runway.

Help me, Lord! Desperately she gasped for breath.

"Where's Matty?" she forced the words painfully through her lips.

Frank blinked.

"The baby?" he snapped. "He's no use to me now! Thanks to you! I'll never convince anyone he's mine now."

Did that mean the DNA test had come through?

Thank You, God. Please let me live long enough to see Matty again.

And Justin.

Frank shifted his grip so that his right forearm pressed against her throat, pinning her to the wall. With his left hand he pulled out his phone and pushed a button.

"I'm not joking around!" he shouted. "I've got the girl cop, and I'm going to hurt her and kill her if this plane doesn't get off the ground!"

And if Matty wasn't on the plane, she wasn't about to be, either. What Justin had told her about walloping his attacker's knee with a rock flashed into her mind. She kicked Frank's right knee as hard as he could. Frank bellowed in pain and stumbled back. The phone clattered to the floor.

Violet pushed past him, feeling so weak she almost fell to her knees. She ran for the door, yanked the handle and shoved it open. Tarmac whizzed past her as the plane accelerated. If she jumped, would she survive the fall? Maybe not, but she was sure that if she stayed, she wouldn't survive the flight.

Frank grabbed her around the waist and yanked her back. She wrenched her arm around and elbowed him in the jaw. She felt the wheels leave the ground only to bounce back down on the runway. But she knew next time they left the ground there might be no going back.

Violet ran for the door again. Then she saw two

bright white headlights shining in the darkness. The truck was racing up the runway toward her.

"Violet!" Justin shouted. Then she saw him. He was crouched in the back of the truck bed, like a knight riding to her rescue. "Hold on! I'm coming!"

Frank grabbed her by the hair and pulled her back from the door again. She screamed in pain and thrashed until she broke his hold.

"Anthony!" Justin shouted. "Pull up alongside the plane and keep it steady."

The small jet began to lift off the tarmac again. Frank snatched up his glass, smashed it against the wall and held the jagged remains before her eyes.

"Stop it!" Frank shouted. "Or I'll kill you!"

A single gunshot rang out behind her, then Frank jerked as a bullet pierced his shoulder. She looked back.

Justin's face appeared through the open door. His gun was still smoking in his hands.

"Jump!" Justin shouted. "I'll catch you!"

The plane began to rise. Violet ran for Justin. He holstered his weapons and raised his hands. She leaped for him through the open door, and in an instant felt Justin's strong arms wrap around her. They tumbled back together into the truck bed.

"We've got her!" Justin banged twice on the cab's back window to signal Anthony.

The plane took off and soared into the sky. The truck slowed beneath them as Anthony eased it to a stop. Gingerly she and Justin pulled themselves up to sit. His strong arm was wrapped around her shoulder. Her hand grabbed the fingers of his other arm and held them tight.

"Hey." His voice was husky. "Are you okay?"

"I think so. How's Matty?"

"Good. Safe, forever. The DNA came through, and Sadie did, too. There are about a billion law enforcement vehicles hiding just out of sight right now. Matty's in one of them with Tessa."

"How did you find me?" she asked.

"A lot of help. Don the bush pilot was the one who finally located which private airfield Frank planned to use. Apparently, Frank tried to brag to Don's wife about hiring a plane, and Missy remembered enough details to put together where his plane was."

A small cry filled the night air. She looked to see Tessa running across the tarmac toward them, with Matty in her arms. Tears of joy filled Violet's eyes. Justin turned and reached for him over the side of the truck. Tessa slid the baby into his arms, and Justin pulled him onto his lap between him and Violet. She reached down and kissed Matty's soft head.

Her heart swelled with more love than she'd ever known possible for one person to hold.

Lord, please bless Justin. Take care of him and give him everything he wants in life. Uphold him and strengthen him. Make all his dreams come true. Help his nephew grow up strong, safe, protected and loved.

Anthony hopped out of the truck. He had his phone to his ear, and by the sound of things he was on with Zablocie. An array of blue-and-red emergency vehicles approached them from across the tarmac, and this time she knew they were on her side. But for a moment she just sat there, with her shoulder leaning against Justin's, side by side in the back of the truck like they had when they used to date.

"The military has scrambled to force the plane down," Anthony said. "He won't get far. Violet, when you're ready, Zablocie wants to speak with you. And yes, he has been un-suspended."

"I'll take it now." Violet started to slide down toward the end of the truck.

"One second." Justin reached for Violet's hand. "Don't go far, okay? Please?"

His eyes searched her face. His fingers linked with hers. And she wondered if his mind was compiling the same list of jobs that needed to be done that hers was. There'd be warrants, interviews and processing the Du-Bois cabin...

"I don't want to just walk from you like nothing's changed between us," Justin added. "I was wrong to let you go, and I don't want to make that mistake again."

"I know. But we can't do this now. This isn't the time or the place."

"But I have to tell you that I—"

"Don't say it." Violet held up her hand, and his voice fell still. "I don't want either of us to say anything right now. I don't want us to profess our feelings and make promises to each other in the middle of a hurricane. Not this time. Whatever I'm feeling for you and whatever you're feeling for me deserves time to breathe, before we can figure out if it's even real."

Justin's head shook. "But I don't want you to think I'm running away from us again."

"I know," Violet said, "and you're not the one walking away this time. I am. Because last time I didn't give you my whole heart, and I didn't get yours in return. And I'm not about to make that same mistake again."

The sun sat high in a bright blue January sky as Justin looked out the window to see Violet's car pull into the driveway of his small two-bedroom bungalow. He watched as his sister Sadie ran across the driveway and gave Violet a long hug, and a huge, beautiful smile spread across Violet's face. Then Sadie got into her social worker's car and left, while Violet picked up two medium pizzas off the front seat of her car and carried them toward the house. Justin met her at the front door.

"Your timing is perfect. My sister was just leaving. I'm so glad she got to see you."

"I'm glad I got to see her. She looks like she's doing really well."

"She is." Justin took the two pizzas—one pepperoni and one Hawaiian—and set them on the table. Then he reached to help her with her coat. "She tells me she's eight days sober and really likes the facility she's living in. It's one day at a time, but I'm hopeful. We've just finalized the adoption papers. I'm going to have full custody of the baby and be his father." Joy swelled in Justin's chest as he said the words. "She's going to have visitation rights." He felt a grin cross his face. "Also, we've chosen a name. Rocky."

"Rocky?" Violet repeated. "Well, that's a strong name for a kid from a strong family."

"It wasn't my first choice." Justin chuckled. "But Sadie really likes it, and it reminds me of the mountains."

Violet laughed. He realized just how much he'd missed her smile. Her hair was back to the same dark beautiful bob that framed the lines of her face. Her indigo eyes shone through thick-rimmed glasses. Something tightened in his chest. He wasn't sure what to think when she'd called him up and asked if he was free for lunch. All he knew was that he was really happy she had.

"And where is Rocky now?"

"Asleep in his cot in my room," Justin said. "I still haven't painted the nursery and was hoping you'd help me pick out a paint color."

"What are the options?"

"Blue and yellow. Maybe green. I've dabbed samples all over the wall."

"Why not do more than one color? I've taken the whole afternoon off. We can go buy paint, if you want, and get a start on it today."

A start. He liked the sound of that.

He and Violet had seen each other dozens of times in countless meetings and calls in the past ten days since they'd rescued Matty from Frank's clutches. The plane had been brought safely down before it had left Canadian airspace, and both Frank and Curly—who turned out to be a hired killer known as Kudryavy—had been arrested. Justin and the Cybercrime Unit had already located several Little Blossoms operatives, and Violet was working with an international task force to take them down and bring all the kidnapped children home safely. A search of the DuBois' cabin had turned up rodenticide in the hot chocolate Frank had given Emelia and Ariel. Emelia had regained consciousness, but due to the extent of her poisoning her lawyers were working out a plea deal that would see her serving her sentence in a medical care facility. Ariel had made a full recovery, taken a plea deal and was working closely with police. Turned out she hadn't known the child was purchased and had believed Little Blossoms was a charity that had rescued the child from a dangerous situation. But perhaps the biggest surprise of all had been that Lorenzo had put together a bid to buy Mount Prince Wilderness Resort from Ross Halton and restore the camp to something he could be proud of. Last Justin had heard, Gloria and her husband, Don and Missy, Toby and Carol, and even Quinn and Jeff of Dukes Wilderness Adventures, who'd given them their cover, had all expressed interest in investing.

And yet, for all the conversations they'd had about the case, this was the first time that he and Violet had actually been alone in a room.

He took a deep breath, reached for her hand and looped his fingers through hers.

"I'm happy you're here, and I don't want to ruin this moment. But I have to be honest with you. No more secrets. No more hiding what I'm feeling. The truth is I'm still in love with you, Violet. You're the most incredible person I know, and I want you in my life, even just as a friend if we can't be something more. I don't want to lose you again."

She stepped toward him and took his other hand in hers.

"I want to elope with you."

His eyes widened. "What?"

"I'm in love with you, too. I want to be your wife, your best friend and the mother of your children. But I don't want to plan another wedding. I just want you as my husband and partner. Today, every day and forever."

He swallowed hard. Then he wrapped his arms around her waist, pulled her to him and buried his face in her hair.

"I want that, too," he whispered. "More than you'll ever know. But we'll have to get a new marriage license. The last one expired."

She laughed and kissed his lips so quickly it surprised him.

"So first we eat pizza, then we go buy paint—"

"When Rocky wakes up from his nap," he added.

"—and then get a marriage license."

"Sounds like a plan." He tightened his arms around her waist and tugged her closer. "But, you know, marriage licenses only last three months."

She pulled back and looked into his eyes. "Justin, I'm not willing to wait three days to marry you."

Then he kissed her. She kissed him back and Justin knew he'd found the woman who'd be his love, his partner and his shelter from the storm for the rest of their lives.

* * * * *

Dear Reader,

Just a quick note this time to thank you for all the happiness and joy you bring into my life. I think about you every day, hoping the stories I write and characters I create make you smile, bring you joy and fill you with hope and confidence to be the person God called you to be.

Thank you for sharing this journey with me,
Maggie

COMING NEXT MONTH FROM
Love Inspired Suspense

ALASKAN WILDERNESS RESCUE
K-9 Search and Rescue • by Sarah Varland

A search for a missing hiker goes disastrously wrong when K-9 search and rescuer Elsie Montgomery and pilot Wyatt Chandler find themselves stranded on a remote Alaskan island. Only they're not alone. But is this a rescue mission...or a deadly trap?

DANGEROUS TEXAS HIDEOUT
Cowboy Protectors • by Virginia Vaughan

When her daughter is the only witness able to identify a group of bank robbers, Penny Jackson knows their lives are in danger. Escaping to a small Texas town was supposed to be safe, but now they must rely on police chief Caleb Harmon to protect them from a killer bent on silencing them...

DEADLY MOUNTAIN ESCAPE
by Mary Alford

Attempting to find a kidnapped woman and expose a human trafficking ring nearly costs Deputy Charlotte Walker her life. But rancher Jonas Knowles saves her, and they work together to locate the others who have been abducted. Can they survive the onslaught of armed criminals *and* the perilous wilderness?

TARGETED FOR ELIMINATION
by Jill Elizabeth Nelson

A morning jog becomes an exercise in terror when Detective Jen Blackwell is ambushed—until her ex-boyfriend Tyler Cade rescues her. Only someone is targeting them both, forcing Jen to team up with the park ranger to uncover the mystery behind the attacks...before it costs them their lives.

WYOMING ABDUCTION THREAT
by Elisabeth Rees

There's only one thing stopping Sheriff Brent Fox from adopting his foster children: his adoption caseworker. But Carly Engelman has very good reasons for caution—all of which disappear when the children's ruthless biological father returns to abduct his kids...with revenge and murder on his mind.

SILENCING THE WITNESS
by Laura Conaway

Avery Sanford thought she was safe in witness protection...until her photo was leaked in the local paper. Now vengeful cartel members are on her tail and only former army commander Seth Brown can help her. But with assailants anticipating their every move, can Avery trust Seth to keep her alive long enough to testify?

LOOK FOR THESE AND OTHER LOVE INSPIRED BOOKS WHEREVER BOOKS ARE SOLD, INCLUDING MOST BOOKSTORES, SUPERMARKETS, DISCOUNT STORES AND DRUGSTORES.

LISCNM1223

Get 3 FREE REWARDS!

We'll send you 2 FREE Books <u>plus</u> a FREE Mystery Gift.

FREE
Value Over
$20

Both the **Love Inspired®** and **Love Inspired® Suspense** series feature compelling novels filled with inspirational romance, faith, forgiveness and hope.

HARLEQUIN
PLUS

Try the best multimedia subscription service for romance readers like you!

Read, Watch and Play.

Experience the easiest way to get the romance content you crave.

Start your **FREE TRIAL** at
<u>www.harlequinplus.com/freetrial</u>.